The pretty blonde h
for weeks stood righ

"I'm Nick. Nick Callahan," he said. He offered his hand.

She took it, and it was warm to the touch. Had she been sunning herself? *Sweet hell. This assignment was going to kill him.*

"I'm Kim Cassidy," she said. "I have the apartment next door. Welcome to Magnolia Falls. Will you be staying long?"

"I'm not sure yet. Depends on how long my business takes, and then… Well, they owe me some time off. Seems like a nice, quiet place." He shrugged.

"It is a nice place, and friendly," she said.

Friendly? Was she going to be friendly? And what did this girl-next-door beauty think friendly entailed? Please, please, don't let this assignment take awhile, he thought. If she got friendly, he just might not be able to take it.

Dear Reader,

No harm has come to any animal during the writing of this book. Promise.

The cat is fine. The cat is now lounging at my feet, sprawled out on his side, his big, furry belly full of expensive, prescription cat food. The cat is happy and ready to be made famous by being in his mom's book.

There are few truly sacred rules to writing, but one of them is: No animal must die.

And none did.

So please do not be alarmed when the cat comes into the picture and startles the hero. It's all a big misunderstanding, and I promise, the cat wins the battle in the end.

The cat is also hilariously vindictive toward the hero. He'll be sorry he ever messed with the cat.

So sit back, relax and don't worry.

The cat is fine.

Teresa Hill

MR. RIGHT NEXT DOOR

TERESA HILL

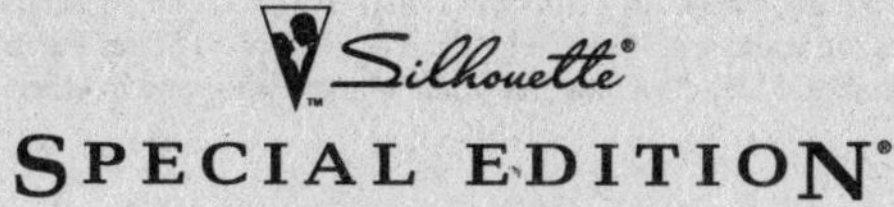

Published by Silhouette Books
America's Publisher of Contemporary Romance

ISBN-13: 978-0-373-24829-2
ISBN-10: 0-373-24829-6

MR. RIGHT NEXT DOOR

This edition published by arrangement with Harlequin Books S.A.

Visit Silhouette Books at www.eHarlequin.com

Printed in U.S.A.

Books by Teresa Hill

Silhouette Special Edition

Magic in a Jelly Jar #1390
(under the name Sally Tyler Hayes)
Heard It Through the Grapevine #1546
A Little Bit Engaged #1740
Her Sister's Fiancé #1793
Mr. Right Next Door #1829

Silhouette Romantic Suspense
(under the name Sally Tyler Hayes)

Whose Child is This? #439
Dixon's Bluff #485
Days Gone By #549
Not His Wife #611
Our Child? #671
Homecoming #700
Temporary Family #738
Second Father #753
Wife, Mother...Lover? #818
†*Dangerous To Love* #903
†*Spies, Lies and Lovers* #940
†*Cinderella and the Spy* #1001
†*Her Secret Guardian* #1012

†Division One

TERESA HILL

lives in South Carolina with her husband, son and daughter. A former journalist for a South Carolina newspaper, she fondly remembers that her decision to write and explore the frontiers of romance came at about the same time she discovered, in junior high, that she'd never be able to join the crew of the *Starship Enterprise*.

Happy and proud to be a stay-home mom, she is thrilled to be living her lifelong dream of writing romances.

For the real Khleo, who lay under my feet,
hoping I'd rub his belly with my toes,
while I wrote most of this book.

My daughter insists everyone know he's a male cat,
spells his name Khleo and is a sweet,
gentle soul, without a violent or vindictive bone
in his giant, furry body.

And for his brother, Inky,
who we call our $900 kitty, after his stay
at the Emergency Vet's last Christmas.

Chapter One

Kim Cassidy grinned like crazy as she made her way off the plane at the Atlanta airport and into the arms of an exasperated-looking blond giant of a man who happened to be her brother.

Jackson Cassidy was gorgeous, solid as they came and most definitely mad.

"Are you trying to make me old before my time?" Jax demanded, crushing her to him for a long moment.

"No, I am not trying," she said, hugging him in return before easing back to smile at him. "And you? Been flashing your badge around again?"

"What if I have?" he said, completely unrepentant, as he waved off the contingent of airport security waiting three paces behind him. "I've got it from here, guys. She's not going to get away from me."

Kim laughed.

"Come along quietly, miss, and I won't get out the handcuffs," he said, hustling her away from the gate.

Kim's fellow passengers, many of whom she'd chatted with on the plane from Heathrow, looked aghast. Airport security understandably looked annoyed. She'd been met at the gate like this more than once, having an unfortunate tendency to run into trouble when traveling. Not that it had been all trouble this time.

"Honestly, baby girl, pirates?" he said, taking her tote bag from her and throwing it over his shoulder.

She giggled, couldn't help it.

"Pirates?" he repeated, louder this time and sounding even more irate.

"Just a couple," she said.

"That's not what I heard."

And, knowing him, he'd heard all about it by now. He probably knew more about the incident than she did, even though she'd been there and he'd been thousands of miles away.

It was truly annoying at times, sweet at others.

"It was not my fault," she insisted. "I was minding my own business, doing nothing more dangerous than sunning myself on the pool deck of the ship. That's it. Just lying there sipping my froufrou drink with one of those cute little umbrellas sticking out of it, when..."

Her cruise ship was attacked by pirates!

It was nearly impossible to believe.

She won a trip on a luxury cruise ship and what happened?

Attacked by modern-day pirates?

Who knew?

Leave it to her to find—on vacation—a disaster of the sort she'd thought had been extinct for hundreds of years.

"I mean...come on?" she tried. "Did you know there were

still pirates floating around looking for ships to hijack? I didn't know. How was I supposed to know?"

Looking no less worried or annoyed, Jax flipped open his cell phone and hit Speed Dial. As they continued to walk, he put the phone to his ear and said, "Got her. All in one piece, too.... Yeah, we'll be there in an hour and a half if I use my sirens."

"There's no need for sirens," she insisted, trying to take the phone from him, but he just frowned down at her, flipped it shut and put it away, which meant he intended to interrogate her all by himself on the ride home without anyone getting in the way.

"Hey, I could still pull out the handcuffs," he said.

"Do it and you won't get a word from me about my trip or the guy I met there," she threatened.

That got his attention. "There's a guy?"

She nodded, her grin back full force as she looked up at him.

"Jax..." she sighed, knowing her voice had taken on a silly, dreamy quality and simply unable to help it. "I think... No, I'm sure. I'm absolutely sure that I'm in love!"

He looked completely taken aback for a moment, stopped dead in his tracks, the line of airline passengers behind them coming to a grumbling halt, some cursing softly as they made their way around her and him, all in a hurry to get somewhere.

"Okay, just...tell me he's not one of the pirates?" he asked with a look that said he couldn't handle that right now.

"No!"

"'Cause that could definitely give me gray hairs. That would be cause for handcuffs and sirens and maybe a jail cell—and you know I could arrange it—until you came to your senses."

"He is not a pirate! He's the guy who saved me from the pirates." She beamed just thinking about it.

"Oh," her brother said, finally giving in to the grumbling

of the crowd now flowing around them and starting to walk again. "A cop?"

"No."

"Rent-a-cop?" His disdainful label of anyone who worked security but wasn't a real cop.

"No," Kim said.

"Soldier?" he tried.

"No. Nothing like that. He was just there and... He was wonderful. He made sure I was completely safe and he even helped fight off the attack. It was amazing, really. You're going to love him."

"So that means I get to meet him, right? Preferably sooner than later?"

"Of course. He's meeting me here in a few days, as soon as he gets back home—"

"Which is where?"

"California—"

"California? I don't like him," her brother insisted.

"You haven't even met him. You can't dislike him just because he's from California."

"Sure I can."

They made it into the wide hallway connecting the main terminal to Baggage Claim, which was packed as usual, and headed toward the down escalator. Kim leaned back against her brother as they rode down.

"Jax? Come on. Don't be like that." She'd known from the start that he'd hate the idea of anyone taking her as far away from the family as California. Not that she wasn't a bit apprehensive about that part herself.

Her family meant a lot to her, her brother and his wife, two older sisters and their husbands, one absolutely adorable two-year-old niece, a baby nephew, the teenager her oldest sister and husband had adopted and two more teens they were foster-parenting at the moment.

Their family life was rich, full and happy, more so than she'd ever thought it could be after losing their beloved mother to cancer four years ago and losing their father, also a cop, when Kim was just two years old.

How could she ever walk away from them?

"That's it. I don't like him. You'll just have to fall for a local guy," her brother said, looking more worried than he had been about the ridiculous pirates who'd tried to board her ship and rob them.

"Serves you right," she claimed. "All those years of you making it so difficult for me to date locally... You should have known there'd be consequences one day."

Jax frowned at that. He was overprotective to a fault at times, but he thought, when he wasn't really annoying her, she could understand why. It couldn't have been easy, taking over as surrogate father to three little girls when he'd been all of eleven years old when their father died.

Still, Kim was twenty-four years old now, something he couldn't quite grasp in moments like this. It was time for him to back off.

"Just don't be a jerk to him when he shows up, all right?" Kim asked as they found the luggage carousel for her flight, still empty at the moment, and stood there to wait.

"I won't be a jerk—"

"And don't try to scare him."

"If he's tough enough to save you from pirates, he should for damned sure be able to handle one older brother with a gun," Jax said.

"No threatening him. And no dragging him off into the woods and beating him up, like you did with Joe." Her middle sister, Kathie's, husband. They'd had a rocky start, especially with her brother.

"I never beat him up in the woods," Jax insisted.

"Just threatened him there?"

"Yeah. I just threatened him there."

"And beat him up at the bank," Kim quipped.

Jax gave her an exasperated look. "We've all moved on from there. You should, too."

"I just don't want anything to go wrong when he shows up."

Because she was fairly certain that he was it.

The one.

The guy she'd been waiting her whole life to find.

It had been a little crazy with him on the ship after the attack. The whole thing had been a classic whirlwind romance, granted, but still…

Beside her, her brother gave a heavy sigh.

Kim linked her arm with his. "You're going to tell me I can't possibly fall in love in a week?"

"No, I was going to let Kate do that."

Older sister. Impossibly practical until she fell in love inside of six weeks herself. Would Kate think it was impossible to do in a week? Kim wasn't sure.

"Hey, you didn't even tell me his name," her brother said.

"No, I didn't."

"You're not even going to tell us his name?"

"Why? So you can run him through the FBI's computer?"

Her brother shrugged, like there was nothing unreasonable about him doing that to everyone she dated.

"Then no, I'm not going to tell you his name," she said, just to annoy him even more.

"Looks sweet as can be, doesn't she?" a tinny voice quipped through what looked like an ordinary, blue-tooth headset that agent Nick Cavanaugh wore, as he followed the woman through the Atlanta airport.

"Find out yet how the guy got through security to meet her at the gate?" Nick said, speaking into the mike of the headset.

It was a really nice break, everyone using those little wireless receivers to talk into their cell phones these days. No more needing to hide a mike and an earpiece discreetly on his body. He just had to look like a guy who was always on the phone.

Technology was absolutely grand.

"Come on, Nick. Don't tell me you haven't noticed how fine that woman looks. Eye candy of the sweetest variety. I mean, yum," Harry said, his voice piped directly into Nick's ear. "You're not dead yet, are you?"

"Not yet," Nick admitted, although his right shoulder was killing him from a nasty little mishap on the ship.

"Don't tell me you didn't even notice how she looks. Somebody said you were surveilling her in a bikini for hours on the ship. Man, I don't know if my heart could have taken it."

"What can I say? That's why they pay me the big bucks," Nick said.

Because he could supposedly handle the sight of sweet little things like her in a bikini and still keep his mind on his job.

"So...how'd the guy with her get through security to meet her at the gate?" Nick asked again.

"Claimed he was a cop."

"She's got a local cop waiting to pick her up as she gets off the plane?" What had the woman done before she'd left town to go on her expensive vacation?

"Yeah, but you didn't see the greeting the cop got as she got off the plane. He did not show up to arrest her."

"Oh," Nick said.

"Yeah. Give us a minute. We're checking right now to see if he's really a cop or not."

"Okay," Nick said and kept walking.

"So maybe she's not as sweet and innocent as she looks, huh?" Harry said. "She's got the guy on the cruise who was just a little vacation fling and her regular guy waiting for her at home?"

"Don't know, Harry."

It was certainly not what they hoped to find when they'd decided at the last minute to tail her as she'd left the ship.

She and the blond guy with a badge stopped dead in the middle of the busy corridor filled with travelers and their luggage, the move so abrupt that Nick had no choice but to keep walking. He'd go pick up a newspaper at the store fifteen feet down and to the right, wait for them to move on and then…

He slipped right past them and…

Ahhh.

It was a sound a man might make when he'd accidentally touched a hot stove. Like he'd been burned.

That's how it felt. *Burning.*

He'd gotten a little too close.

And with her, it mattered.

He'd actually touched her, brushed past her right shoulder as she'd turned her hair at just the right moment. A wave of pretty, blond curls had teased their way past his nose, just out of reach but leaving him with a giant whiff of her.

And she smelled really good.

He'd found that out on the ship, too.

The woman smelled great, looked… Well, it was scary what that woman could do to a little, yellow bikini. It was downright unfair. Criminal, even.

He had indeed been forced to watch her for hours sunning herself in a bikini. She'd rubbed lotion on herself and he'd watched. Drank a silly, fruity drink, licking her lips when she was done, and he'd watched. Rolled over onto a perfectly toned tummy and then reached behind her back to untie the strings of her top, baring a completely naked back, while he watched and another agent had been whispering in his ear, speculating about how much Nick and the rest of the crew would pay him to dump a cup of ice water on her back and make her jump up, leaving the top behind.

Nick had watched it all.

There'd been a secluded deck on the ship reserved for nude sunbathing. He would be forever grateful she hadn't gone there and taken any more of her little suit off.

But now he'd gotten close enough to smell her hair, actually brush past her shoulder, and every other thought—except what torment she'd already caused him—had simply vanished from his head.

"Hey, what did she say?" Harry asked.

Nick had no earthly idea.

Damn.

"I think it was something about being in love," Harry said.

Nick frowned. Love was not an emotion he wanted involved in any of his cases. Lust was trouble enough, especially when it was him lusting after a pretty woman in a bikini, but love… Love was bad. It was awful. People who thought they were in love did completely unpredictable, illogical, often incredibly stupid things. They got mad. They got hurt. They set out for revenge, ruining their lives and often the lives of people around them, all in the name of that foolish thing called love.

God save him from another woman in love.

"Did you get that on tape?" Nick asked. "Can you play it back?"

"Yeah, hang on. It'll be up in a second or two. We'll up the volume on the playback for you. Here it comes."

There was a lot of background noise, but he knew her voice by now, just as well as he knew how she smelled.

He might try to fool the other guys working with him on this case, but he wasn't going to try to fool himself. It was hard not to remember the woman's sweet, slow, genuine-sounding Southern drawl. He'd fallen into an exhausted, all-too-brief sleep the last two nights with the sound of her voice and the things she'd said running through his head.

The way she laughed.

The pretty smile she so often flashed.

The twinkle in her pretty blue eyes.

And yes, the way she'd looked in that little, yellow string bikini.

Contrary to popular belief, he was not inhuman, just disciplined and focused most of the time, better than most at hiding any feelings he might be unfortunate enough to have and suspicious as hell of almost anyone he met, especially a pretty woman who might or might not be innocent of whatever crime he happened to be investigating.

Okay, there it was, the tape of the conversation she'd had not thirty seconds ago, playing in his head, the way her voice had been doing for the last forty-eight hours already.

"I think…" she said. "No…" The tape cut in and out. "Sure…" Come on. Let 'em hear it. "I'm in love."

"Oh, great," Nick said.

"Yeah, baby," Harry said. "What do you think? From the way our guy was hanging all over her the last few days, it's gotta be him, right?"

"Hell, I don't know. You know how women are, Harry."

Nick had to hope one Eric Weyzinski didn't feel the same way. That he wouldn't have a little fling with someone like her on a ship and just walk away from her when it was over.

He had to hope Weyzinski was either coming here, or she was going to him, so Nick could follow her and find Weyzinski again. Because they'd screwed up as the ship's passengers left, lost Weyzinski and they still hadn't figured out whether he was their bad guy or not.

That was Nick's job.

Catching the bad guys.

Catch 'em and move on.

That was his motto, his life, and it suited him just fine.

One crook after the next.

Bring 'em on.

"Okay," Harry said through his earpiece. "The guy with her did flash a badge to get through security. From a police force in a little town north of the city called Magnolia Falls, which is where our pretty blonde claims to live. We'll check with the cops there and get back to you to tell you for sure if he is who he claims he is. And from the information I've got now, looks like he and our blonde have the same last name. Cassidy. His name is Jackson Cassidy."

"Tell me she's not his wife," Nick said.

Because the thing people thought was love, coupled with a marriage license and a wedding ring, mixed in with jealousy and another man who happened to be a crook… That was sure to be a disaster in the making.

"If the cop's her husband, she wouldn't come home from vacation alone and announce to him that she's in love with someone else," Harry reminded him.

"Oh, she just might." He'd seen more than one unhappy wife throw something like that in her husband's face.

"Hey, buddy, remember that little problem of yours we've talked about before? The woman thing?"

"I don't have a problem with women," he claimed. "I just have women who happen to cause me problems quite often."

Her being merely the latest in a long string of problem-causing women.

"But I don't have a problem with women," Nick insisted.

"All right, buddy. Whatever you say. What's your pretty blonde doing now?"

"Well, the cop looks unhappy about her little announcement, but not pissed off. So I'd say he's not her husband."

One thing to be grateful for.

"Okay," Harry said. "Didn't think so."

"Hang on. We're moving again," Nick said, putting down the newspaper he'd picked up moments ago and falling into step behind them, blending into the crowd as best he could.

They made it to the escalator and he managed to get a spot right behind her by rudely cutting in front of an older couple and a woman with a baby, jostling his sore shoulder as he went.

Oh well.

A guy had to do what a guy had to do.

So what if the shoulder still hurt when all he'd done was taken a fall and rolled through it? So what if he didn't roll as well as he used to and he grew more cynical by the moment?

He could still do the job better than most.

And he was not old.

Thirty-eight was not old for an agent.

Thirty-eight meant he was simply more experienced and therefore smarter than most.

Knew all about women and love.

And this was nothing but another job.

With the kind of discipline his job demanded, he put his focus firmly back on his case. They had a band of modern-day pirates based off the northern coast of Africa preying on passing vessels. Private boats at first, the crooks stealing to fund whatever other things they might be doing. Then they'd moved on to bigger and better things. Luxury yachts and, now, cruise ships.

How the hell did they expect to actually board a cruise ship?

Nick didn't know, but if they ever did, the potential consequences were enormous.

Hostage-taking? Massive ransom demands? Terrorism?

Nick didn't even want to think of what they might do if they weren't stopped soon.

His agency had gotten a tip that the luxury liner *The Paradigm* was the group's next target, and he'd been on board since the ship docked in Rome eight days ago.

There'd been more than a thousand passengers, plus a crew of over six hundred on its maiden voyage. The pretty, young blonde he was following had been one of them. The guy she'd been hanging out with might have been in league with the pirates—on board in advance to help them take control of the ship—or he might not have been. Nick didn't know yet. They hadn't focused on Weyzinski until very late in the game. There'd simply been too many possible suspects to check them all quickly. By the time they'd grown suspicious of Weyzinski, the cruise had been nearly over. Then Weyzinski had managed to give another agent the slip as he'd left the ship.

Which meant one of the few leads they still had to Weyzinski was the pretty blonde, supposedly one Kimberly Ann Cassidy of a little town called Magnolia Falls, Georgia.

They'd been scrambling just to follow her, to get Nick on her plane for the States and get agents in place waiting for her in the Atlanta airport when she arrived. They didn't even know yet if Kim Cassidy was her real name. They didn't know if she was working with Weyzinski or just an innocent victim.

Nick had to find out.

He followed her and the cop through the baggage-claim

area until they stopped at an empty carousel. He hoped he'd at least have time to grab his checked bag before she found hers and took off.

"My car's waiting at the curb?" Nick asked, knowing Harry would have tried to arrange things that way.

"It's there. Bright red Lexus convertible. Sorry about the color, but the car will flat-out fly if you need it to. Try not to hurt it, okay?"

Nick sighed. "That was not my fault, Harry."

A car chase on a freeway near L.A. six months ago had ended badly and he was still catching hell for it. Nick's right knee had plowed into the dashboard. It still bothered him at times, usually when it rained.

"I don't suppose you can get someone to hold her bag in the back for a while?"

"We're working on it. Sorry, buddy. I didn't get here until fifteen minutes before her plane touched down. But I'm getting a sheet on the cop right now. Okay… Looks like he is her brother."

"Okay. So she wasn't two-timing him with the guy on the ship."

One point in her favor.

And if she was announcing that she was in love like that, as she arrived home from her trip, odds are it was with Weyzinski.

"Yeah, here's the brother's driver's license photo and hers. Definitely the same guy who's with her now. Looks like he's been on the force for seven years now. Somebody talked to his supervisor in Magnolia Falls. Tried to make it all sound routine, but I don't know, Nick. Maybe the department just didn't like the idea of him flashing his badge around the airport without them knowing anything about it. Could be that. Could be something else. But they definitely didn't like someone asking questions about one of their guys."

Okay, so it looked like he wouldn't be asking for cooperation from the local law enforcement agencies anytime soon. And he was going to be tailing a cop's sister.

No problem.

"Don't see any red flags on his service record, except something about a brawl in a bank a couple of years ago," Harry said. "Wait… Damn."

"What is it?"

"Their father was a cop. Shot and killed trying to stop a convenience-store robbery when our blonde was just a baby."

Great.

Cops took care of their own. They took care of the families of cops. And more than anything else, they took care of the families of fallen officers.

Harry started laughing.

"Oh jeez, Nick. Are you ready for this? The town is all of twenty-four-hundred people. You're entering a different world, my friend. You will not fit in well."

"You don't know that," Nick argued. "I can fit in anywhere."

Small-town America.

How hard could it be?

He'd blend with the best of 'em.

"She's lived there her entire life," Harry continued.

"So everybody knows her. Should be easy to get information on her."

"If you can get 'em to talk."

"I can get anybody to talk," Nick boasted.

"She has not only the brother, but two sisters. Our pretty blonde is the baby of the family." Harry laughed. "Looks like she's been babied her whole life, doesn't she?"

Nick felt an odd little kick in the gut at that.

A pretty, impossibly young pampered blonde who looked

like a million bucks in a yellow string bikini, and who was probably used to getting her way in everything, indulged in every whim. God help him.

"Oh, man. All three of her siblings are married and living right there in Magnolia Falls," Harry said. "This will not be good."

Nick sighed.

Okay, so it didn't sound good.

A cop for a brother, dead cop for a father.

A ton of relatives.

A tiny town.

A whole police force that would be looking out for her if anyone got wind of what Nick was doing in town.

Harry laughed some more.

"Guess what she does?"

"No clue," Nick said, but he wasn't going to like it. He could already tell.

"Elementary school art teacher. Isn't that sweet?"

Nick swore.

He had a nice, maybe sweet, definitely innocent-looking elementary school teacher, the baby of a family of four, the daughter of a slain police officer, in love with a guy Nick was sure was a crook.

And Nick had to use her to find the crook.

"She's gonna love you before you're through," Harry said.

"Yeah."

This was why he got the big bucks.

Making nice, innocent women like her hate him.

Chapter Two

Nick's bag showed up before hers, which meant he wouldn't have to live out of his carry-on.

He could have managed, of course. He could have made it for weeks with nothing more than he could carry in a baggie if he had to. But life was more fun with all his nifty surveillance toys and a man couldn't carry a loaded gun on a plane anymore without a ton of paperwork, which he hadn't had time to produce in his rush to get on the flight. Fortunately, checked baggage was another story.

He grabbed his bag, shouldered his carry-on and tried not to wince at the added pressure to his wounded knee.

Harry must have been close enough to see his expression, because Harry started chuckling and said, "God, you're old, Nick."

Nick suggested several things Harry might do, all of which were probably illegal in this state, then got back to business.

"Tell me you have her, because if you do, I'm going to find my car."

"You'd better because we spotted the brother's patrol car parked illegally at the curb. You need to be ready to move, my friend. We're trying to get another car in place in case you lose 'em."

"I'm not going to lose a small-town cop who doesn't even know I'm following him," Nick protested.

"Yeah, yeah. Just trying to back you up, Nick. That's all. That's my job. To make your job easier."

Nick swore softly then spotted a tiny, expensive-looking convertible that gave the appearance of being capable of flying, and produced his government ID for the young agent standing by the car.

"Here you are, sir," the kid said, holding a briefing report, what little they'd been able to prepare by the time Nick landed.

"Thank you." His bag went into the tiny trunk, the carry-on onto the passenger seat and then, with a kind of exaggerated care that irritated him greatly, Nick managed to fit himself into the driver's seat without crushing his sore knee on the steering wheel or the dashboard, while Harry started laughing again.

"Son of a bitch," Nick said. "You did this on purpose, didn't you?"

"I just figured you'd be happy to sacrifice your own comfort, if necessary, for speed and maneuverability. Was I wrong? I mean, we could look for one of those cars outfitted for special-needs drivers, if we need to. Do you need one of those, Nick?"

"I'll put this sore knee of mine in your gut, Harry, if you need to know how well it still works," he said, though it might have been a pure bluff.

Honestly, he wasn't sure he could manage it. Hours on a plane had left his knee stiff and sore beyond reason. He could just imagine Harry's glee if he called room service that night and asked if they could provide a heating pad for him.

If his pretty blonde gave him any time to relax.

She could have a string of men waiting for her. Weyzinski could already be here, waiting for her. She could be up to all sorts of things that didn't involve teaching little children how to finger paint.

Honestly, how innocent could a woman who looked like that in a bikini possibly be?

Nick started the car and moved the seat all the way back to accommodate his length. He adjusted his mirrors, spotted the small-town cop car, just where Harry said it would be, then checked the car's satellite navigation system, preprogrammed for the destination of Magnolia Falls.

It shouldn't be hard to follow the blonde and her brother. After choosing whether to take the freeway loop around Atlanta or plow straight through downtown, it looked like there was only one real choice of roads that went from the other side of the metro area to Magnolia Falls.

Nick didn't think he'd ever been to a town this small.

"Okay, here they come," Harry told him.

Nick didn't turn his head, following them out of the corner of his eyes. The pretty blonde was laughing, looking as relaxed and happy as could be. Her brother looked like he could cheerfully spit nails.

Nick wondered why.

Of course, if he had a little sister who looked like her, Nick could imagine her giving him headaches. And he'd be none too happy to have her go off on vacation and get attacked by pirates.

The brother's expression could be nothing but that.

And it could be so much more.

She could be a woman constantly getting into trouble of one sort or another. Man trouble. The kind that came from making really bad decisions and not thinking things through. Or from just being young and impulsive.

Innocent.

She could be completely innocent, a victim in all of this.

Nick frowned.

He'd watched her on the ship in a way that had nothing to do with his job, simply hadn't been able to help himself.

The older and more jaded he got, the more he needed to believe that there were still people like her in this world or, at least, people like she appeared to be. Young, innocent, carefree. Happy. Sexy in a sweetly inviting way, nothing cold or calculating in the least about her.

Not that he could imagine her giving him the time of day or him accepting such an offer.

She was not a creature of his world and he wasn't a man of hers. And he'd bet she wasn't the kind of woman to have a quick, thoroughly satisfying fling with a man like him, despite what he'd seen on that ship.

She and her brother got into the police cruiser and pulled out into traffic. Nick followed them, all the while telling himself to treat her as he would any other woman he met in the course of an investigation.

No, to treat her better than that.

To try to stay the hell away from her and not break her heart too badly when he showed her how foolish it was to fall in love with a man she knew nothing about.

Atlanta traffic turned out to be brutal and the cop drove like a bat out of hell. If Nick didn't know better, he would have sworn half the drivers on the freeway had gone through the same defensive-driving training he had.

No, more like offensive-driving training. He'd had that, too, but maybe not as much as the other drivers on the road had.

Damn.

He'd been cut off ruthlessly more times than he could count and when traffic got really annoying, the brother wasn't shy about applying his siren to get out of it, a luxury Nick didn't have.

If Harry had seen him, he'd have howled.

Honestly, the day he couldn't manage to follow a small-town cop successfully was the day he gave up government work and started fishing for a living or contemplating his navel or some other ridiculously worthless form of life.

They made it to Magnolia Falls in an hour and twenty-seven mind-boggling minutes on the road. Truth was, Nick wasn't absolutely sure the brother hadn't picked up on the fact that he was being tailed.

It was sad really, the depths to which Nick's life had sunk.

His knee hurt. He hadn't slept for more than a few hours in two days, and he was as grumpy as…well, as an old man, much as it pained him to admit it.

His pretty blonde was delivered to the address Harry had given him, the one listed on her driver's license.

It turned out to be an old monstrosity of a house that, from her address—2B—he'd guess had been cut up into apartments. Either that or the blonde was clearly not living on a beginning teacher's salary.

Nick parked half a block down the road and watched the brother carry in her bags and then leave. Harry, he knew, would be working on getting a tap on Ms. Kim Cassidy's home phone. With luck, they could zero in on some of her cell phone calls, too. Nick would have backup from a team of agents as soon as they could be put into place, but for the moment, the blonde was all his.

He frowned, thinking about virtually living out of a car this small and what that would do to his screwy knee, thinking of nosy small-town neighbors and being pestered by small-town cops.

Already, he thought a little old lady from the house across the street was staring at him through her front window.

Did these people have nothing else to do other than monitor traffic on the street?

"Harry," he said into the mike in his headset, "I think the old woman across the street's made me. I'm going to have to move."

His knee said so clearly. *Move, move, move.*

"You're in luck. The house next door to the blonde has just been converted into a bed-and-breakfast. I called to try and book a room but they said they're not officially opening until next week. I bet if you're sweet, you can show up at the door and talk them into giving you a room now anyway."

Nick offered up a quick thanks to the universe on behalf of his knee, hoping he hadn't entirely lost his power of sweet-talking. It had never been his strong point and he wasn't feeling even remotely syrupy at the moment. Hell, he never did.

"Tell them you're an early riser and that you'd like a room that gets morning sunshine," Harry said.

"Do I look like a guy who gives a crap about morning sunshine?"

Harry just laughed. "That'll put you on the side of the house facing our pretty blonde's apartment. Get a room on the second floor and you might be able to look in her windows."

No way Nick wanted to look in her windows. He was starting to sweat just thinking about it. And he wondered how long Harry'd known about the B&B but left him sitting in the cramped car. He fought the urge to bang his head against the steering wheel in a general expression of dismay about most everything in his life at the moment, most of all this assignment and the woman upstairs with the innocent eyes and the body that just wouldn't quit.

The one who made him feel about a hundred and sixty years old.

He started his toy of a car and tried to prepare himself for what might pass for sweet talk to the owners of the new B&B.

Nick finger-combed his dark brown hair, which had grown too long for him and was desperately in need of a trim, then ran a hand along his jaw. A shave was definitely in order. Clean clothes, a shower, a real bed…these were the things of his dreams.

If he could just knock out the blonde and ensure that she'd be unconscious for a few hours, he could take a nap, but he really didn't want to try to sneak up behind her and do the Vulcan neck-pinch thing and get caught. Plus, it would definitely put her on the defensive when she woke up and he didn't want that. He wanted her to relax and tell him everything—or at least tell someone in such a way that Nick could eavesdrop on the conversation.

Which meant no Vulcan neck pinch.

No nap anywhere in his near future.

He was grumpy as an old bear.

He grimaced as he started his toy car and peeled off down the street and into the driveway of the B&B.

"Harry, you there?" he said into his headpiece.

"Yeah. Try not to scare the nice people with the nice, soft bed and the hot shower, Nickie."

"Why would I scare them?"

"'Cause you're a scary guy," Harry quipped.

Nick got out of the car, scanning the area even more carefully than before. "Are you looking at me right now, Harry?"

"Why? You see me?"

"No, I haven't spotted you."

"Then I'm not looking at you, Nick."

Shaking his head and swearing, Nick gabbed his carry-on, popped the trunk and pulled out his suitcase, trying not to grimace at the way it pulled tight something deep inside his sore shoulder. *Dammit.*

"So before, you were just guessing about the expression I might have on my face?" Nick asked.

"Nah, just knowing your sweet disposition and thinking about how much we need this room next door to the pretty blonde, that's all. Trying to look out for you, give you some helpful hints to make the job easier."

"Gee, thanks," Nick grumbled, making his way to the front door.

It was made of leaded glass and highly polished oak. A discreet aged-brass plate to the left of the door said, Baker B&B, Main & Vine, Magnolia Falls, Ga.

Okay, he was going to make nice with the Bakers of Baker B&B if it killed him; beg for a shower then spy on their nice neighbor next door.

He put on what he hoped was a mild-mannered but tired-to-the-verge-of-exhausted, plain-old-businessman smile, trying to look nonthreatening and ordinary, definitely not grumpy. Like he'd be no trouble at all as a guest of a not-quite-open B&B.

A woman in sweats, a T-shirt and holding a dust mop answered the door.

Cleaning lady or Mrs. Baker?

He had to decide quick.

He'd insult her if she was Mrs. Baker and he thought she was the cleaning lady and he couldn't insult her and get a room.

"Ma'am," Harry said. "Just say ma'am. It's what all good Southern boys do."

So Harry was watching. The rat.

Still, Harry wouldn't steer him wrong when it came to spying. Nick went with it.

"Ma'am," he said, respectfully tipping his head to her. "Am I too early to get a room?"

"Oh, my." She frowned, then started trying to dust herself, succeeding only in creating a cloud of dust between them. "We're really not open yet. Not until next week."

"That's what I heard in town, but I was hoping I could change your mind. I love old houses. So much charm and character." He managed not to choke on the words. He even, he thought, sounded remotely sincere. "And yours looks so inviting."

"Thank you," she said warily. "It's just that we have so much to get done before we actually open…"

"Oh, I won't get in your way. Not in the least. I'm very self-sufficient. And I don't even eat breakfast—"

"You don't?"

Nick fell silent, not used to strangers asking about his eating habits. He'd only said that to be nice, to make her think he would cause no trouble at all as a guest. Did she expect an answer?

He gleaned from her expression that she did.

"Well…no," he said. "Not usually."

"We all need a good breakfast," she said, taking on a tone he might expect from a maiden aunt, if he had a maiden aunt.

Nick frowned. He might have a maiden aunt. He couldn't quite remember. There were all sorts of relatives on his mother's side of the family who he hardly ever saw. He was doing good if he saw his mother every now and then, let alone anyone else he might be related to.

"We can't have you running around without breakfast all the time. No wonder you look so. Well, so…"

Her words trailed off.

He gathered that she might want to take care of him?

Nick didn't understand. She didn't even know him. Why would she want to take care of him?

Still, this was not a bad thing considering what he wanted from her: a room next to his pretty blonde.

Nick tried to look in need of sympathy and a hot breakfast, but at the same time, like a man who'd cause no trouble at all in an unopened B&B full of dust.

"Tired?" he suggested. "I look tired?"

The woman nodded, as if to say that didn't nearly cover what she thought he looked like.

"Overnight flight from Brazil," he said. "Hate those. Absolutely hate them. Getting way too old for them."

Harry chuckled in his ear.

Nick struggled to show no signs of conversing with two people at once, one of whom the woman couldn't see.

"Honey," she said, "if you're too old, I should be in my grave soon."

To which Nick had no idea what to say.

He stood there looking puzzled, tired but not sickly, he hoped, and in need of sympathy and some kindhearted womanly care, which he thought she could provide if she felt sorry for him, which he hoped she did.

"Still, I really don't know," she began.

"Sure. I understand," he said, telling himself not to beg. "I had a room downtown at the…the…"

"Bluebird Inn," Harry supplied.

There was a Bluebird Inn?

"Bluebird Inn," Nick tried.

"Yes. Lovely place," Mrs. Baker said. "They'll take good care of you—"

"Oh, I'm sure they would have," Nick said. "They just… Well, there was a little problem with the electricity."

"Electricity?" Harry said. "Sure. Okay. We can do that. Power's going out at the Bluebird in minutes. I'm on it."

"They don't have any power," Nick said. Harry could make it true. "Don't know when it'll be back up and they wouldn't let me check in, not knowing if they'd have electricity."

"Oh, well… You poor thing," she said.

Nick tried hard to look like a poor thing.

He feared it wouldn't take much effort.

"On that plane all night and now you don't even have a room," Mrs. Baker said, shaking her head sympathetically. "And you're hurt?"

It was only then that he realized he was rubbing his sore shoulder.

"Oh, it's nothing. Really, ma'am."

Hurt, tired, no room and no breakfast, unless she took him in.

He stood there and let it all sink in.

He could limp a little if he had to.

"Well, we can't leave you in such a sad state with no place to stay," she said. "If you don't care that the place is not quite ready, I guess I don't, either."

Okay.

He was in.

"So, would you happen to have a room that gets morning sun? I'm an early riser, love morning sunshine," he said, trying not to choke on the words as he went inside.

Nick feared he would indeed be able to look into Kim Cassidy's living room window from his room.

God help him.

He tugged on his tie, which was absolutely too tight when he thought about what he might see of her in those windows, in what she believed was the privacy of her own living room.

"You dog," Harry said, when he told him about the view.

Please let her close her blinds very tightly at night. Please.

As it was, he could glance over and see her moving around in there. The blinds were tilted at an angle that would have blocked any view from the street, but the second floor of the B&B was higher than the second floor of her house, and he was afraid the angle coupled with a light being left on inside once it got dark would prove devastating to a man who'd been looking at her for way too long already.

"I've got to get some air," he told Harry, abandoning the unpacking and hiding of his little spy toys, in case he couldn't convince Mrs. Baker not to clean his room.

He bolted from the room, down the stairs, startling her as she swept the kitchen.

"Sorry," he said. "Just need some air."

"Oh, well try the patio. The backyard is glorious this time of year."

"Okay."

Out he went, finding himself on a flagstone patio complete with a wrought iron table and chairs, plus a chaise lounge. He considered collapsing upon the lounge chair, but after doing such a great sell job on being exhausted and hurt, his landlady would probably call EMS for him. So he stayed on his feet, trying not to pace too obviously and maybe muttering to himself. He couldn't quite be sure, just hoped it wasn't classified information coming out of his mouth.

He got to one end of the stone patio, lined with all sorts of blooming things in big stone planters, then pivoted to head in the other direction. Back and forth he went, until he pivoted for the last time and…

Nearly found himself with an armful of woman.

"Ahhh." She caught her breath.

He did, too.

Was he dreaming? Hallucinating? Sleeping right now?

Nick shook his head to clear it, but the image before him remained stubbornly the same.

Her.

His pretty, distracting blonde, right here in front of him.

She tried to back up but couldn't because he held her by her arms. Because he'd been afraid of knocking her over. And then she smiled up at him.

"Hi," she said. "Sorry. I was going to say hi, and then you turned around and…well… Hi."

"Hi," he said, nearly incoherently.

"Oh, yeah. Forgot to tell you," Harry said into his ear. "She's on her way over there."

Harry was such an ass and Nick could not for the life of him figure out where the man was, what possible spot could give him the vantage point he needed to see everything that he'd seen.

The jerk.

In front of him, the pretty blonde's smile faltered, no doubt because of the scowl on Nick's own face.

"I didn't mean to disturb you," she said.

"No. No. It's not that," he said, making himself let go of her. If she wanted to run away from him, he wasn't going to stop her. Hell, he'd probably thank her, despite the job he had to do. "I was just distracted. That's all. Sorry I almost plowed into you."

"I'm fine. Just surprised. I thought you were Sam."

"Sam?"

"Mrs. Baker's nephew. I saw you from the back and you're about the same height and he has brown hair like yours. Although I would have been surprised to see Sam in a suit. Still… Sam's been working in the backyard for weeks, helping to get the B&B ready. I was just going to say hi to him before I went inside to see Mrs. Baker."

She smiled again, stood there with the full light of the sun glinting off her blond curls, her legs bare, her arms, all that golden sun-kissed skin. Not as much as she'd shown off in the yellow bikini, but more than enough to give a man all sorts of ideas.

He'd kept thinking on the ship, as she'd sunned herself, of how warm her skin must be after she laid in the sunshine for so long. How hot she'd be to the touch.

Nick made a face, then tried not to. He'd already nearly scared her away. He just had to stop thinking about her and her skin and touching her. He just needed to spy on her without thinking of her.

How the hell was he supposed to do that?

Into his head came that old Mick Jagger and the Rolling Stones song.

You make a grown man cryyyyy-eeyyyyyyee. Do-do-do-do. You make a grown man cryyyy-eeyyyyyee.

She could definitely make a man cry.

"So…" she said, still looking way too friendly despite his Dr.-Jekyll-and-Mr.-Hyde act. "Did Mrs. Baker open up the B&B while I was gone?"

"She didn't plan on it, but I convinced her to take me in early." He tried to gather up enough scattered brain cells to put together another sentence. *Come on, Nick. She's just a woman, one who's likely in love with a crook at that.* "I'm Nick. Nick Cavanaugh."

He had no choice but to offer his hand and, despite his every wish or maybe because of things he wouldn't even let himself admit he wanted, she took it. He didn't think he was standing there with his mouth hanging open, thinking way too much about having her hand in his, but he couldn't be sure. And yes, even her hand was hot to the touch. Had she been sunning herself and he'd missed it?

"Down, boy," Harry said.

Sweet hell.

This assignment was going to kill him.

"I'm Kim Cassidy. I have an apartment next door. Welcome to Magnolia Falls."

"Thank you."

"Are you staying long?"

"I'm not sure yet. Depends on how long my business takes, and then… Well, they owe me some time off. Seems like a nice, quiet place." He shrugged. Damn, his shoulder hurt. He was falling apart. Whereas she seemed perfectly put together.

"It is a nice place. And friendly," she said.

Friendly? Was she going to be friendly? And just what did she think being friendly entailed?

"I might stay awhile," he said.

Please, please don't let this take a while. Please don't let her get all that friendly. He couldn't take it.

Let her crook of a boyfriend show up tomorrow. Let him get this over with and get out of here and forget all about her and the way he feared she'd look once he was done here.

"Well, I hope you like it. Let me know if you need anything."

"I will," he said, then couldn't let it go at that. He did have a job to do. He couldn't stand to fumble around gawking over her, not if he was going to get the job done. "Actually, I need lunch. A place to have lunch. What's good here in town?"

"That's easy. The Corner Diner on Main. Just go that way." She pointed off to the left. "It's about eight blocks down. You can't miss it. I'm meeting my sisters there in a few minutes, trying to beat the lunch crowd."

"There's a crowd?"

She nodded. "Just about the only one you'll ever see in town. If you want lunch without having to wait, you should go now. I'm going inside to say hello to Mrs. Baker before I head that way myself."

"Okay. I'll give it a try."

"Then I guess I'll see you there," she said, heading up the steps and inside, calling out Mrs. Baker's name and knocking only as she went through the doorway.

So, he was going to lunch and she was going to be there. Hopefully telling her sisters all about her little trip and the guy she'd met.

Nick sighed.

Maybe this would be easy.

Maybe it would be easy and he could finish it up and go home.

"Not bad," Harry said. "Not as smooth as I've seen you, but still…not bad."

"Where the hell are you?" he barked.

Harry just laughed.

Nick headed off to lunch.

To spy on her.

Chapter Three

Nick was happily eating his lunch—meat loaf and mashed potatoes smothered in heart-clogging gravy—when people started screaming.

At least, at first he thought they were screaming.

He nearly pulled out his gun before he realized it wasn't really screaming.

It was more like…squealing.

Happy squealing?

Sounds he wasn't sure he'd ever heard come out of a woman's mouth before in public, maybe not even in the privacy of his own bedroom, and here he was thinking that he could make women make some really interesting, happy sounds.

But there he was, in the Corner Diner in Magnolia Falls, and his prime lead in the case of the pirate ring had just entered the establishment in a rush, thrown open her pretty suntanned arms, embracing three different women at the same time, and all four of them were doing something that could only be described as squealing for joy.

"Good God," Nick muttered, just loud enough for Harry to hear, apparently.

Because the next thing he heard was Harry in his ear saying, "It's a Southern thing. Southern women do that."

"Do they do it in bed?" Nick asked, unable to help himself.

Harry laughed. "If you do it right, Southern women can make all sorts of little sounds like that in bed. 'Course the way you're limping along right now and with that bad back of yours—"

"I don't have a bad back. A shoulder. Just a shoulder—"

"Okay. Shoulder. I don't think you should attempt a move like that, Nickie. I don't want you to hurt yourself, you know?"

"In bed?" he muttered. "The day I can't take a woman to bed without hurting myself is the day I—"

Nick looked up into the half-disapproving, half-amused face of the woman who'd seated him at the diner, the owner herself, Darlene Hodges.

"Sorry," he told her. "I was just…" He gestured feebly at the headset he wore and shrugged.

"No problem, honey. I wouldn't want you to hurt yourself, either." She nodded understandingly. "But just in case, you should know, a man gets to a certain age and all sorts of things just start to go. Women understand these things. At least, some women do. Not that I think you really need to worry all that much."

Harry was howling.

Nick gulped. He had no idea what to say.

"You want some more coffee?" Darlene asked, smiling in that understanding way of hers.

"Sure," Nick said, so that maybe she'd go away and not come back again anytime soon, so that he wouldn't have to decide whether she was flirting with him or making fun of him and his feebleness. He really wasn't sure. He really didn't want to know.

His head hurt. His shoulder and his back hurt. His knee hurt. And he just wanted to go to sleep but was afraid he'd dream about Kim and things a man ten years younger than him might be able to do to her to make her make that sound Nick had never heard before from a woman in bed.

Darlene poured his coffee and walked away.

"That was the funniest damned thing I've heard all week," Harry proclaimed. "Maybe so far this year—"

"Shut up, Harry," Nick said. Then, in disgust over having Harry and his smart-ass comments in his ear, Nick hit a button and cut off the connection. It wasn't like Harry was helping.

Nick sat there, pretending to eat, watching as Kim continued to greet the two women—who had to be her sisters from the resemblance between the three of them—and a petite brunette. Most of the squealing had stopped, but the hugging hadn't and the women were chattering like mad, all at the same time. He couldn't make out anything, really, and he was only two tables away.

He'd spotted her sisters the minute he'd walked into the diner. It was frightening to think there were two other women in the world who looked nearly as good as her. Really scary. Same shade of blond hair, same young, happy, girl-next-door sexy looks. They must have driven the men in this town nuts for years. He was scared to be in the same room with the three of them, but he had to. So Nick planted himself at a table nearby and expected to be able to hear everything. He had very good hearing. Unlike his knee, his hearing wasn't going, yet.

And he was sure there was good stuff to hear. He just couldn't keep up, because he could swear every one of the four women was talking at once. He stared, thinking that looking at them as they talked might make it easier to follow the conversation.

It swirled around him in a practically indistinguishable blob of chatter.

"Really in love—?"

"Knew the minute you saw him—?"

"Just like that—?"

"Scared—?"

"Hear all about the attack—"

"So brave—"

"Protect you—?"

"Ever get home—?"

"Worse than that time in Vienna—?"

Vienna?

What had she done in Vienna?

The pirate ring might have been in Vienna recently. They weren't sure. They were still checking.

Vienna?

Nick had lost at least a dozen lines of dialogue just thinking of it. *Vienna?*

"Can't wait to meet him—"

"Coming here—?"

Wait a minute. What was that?

Had she said *he* was coming here?

Her pirate/terrorist/lover boy?

Did he make her squeal?

"Ahhhh!" Nick closed his eyes and groaned, disgusted to even think his thoughts had gone in that direction—her and the pirate wannabe in bed, her making those sounds, him with too bad a back or shoulder or knee to even think of doing things like that with her or anyone else.

When he opened his eyes again, he saw Darlene and one of the waitresses huddled in the corner looking at him strangely. Like they might be a little bit afraid of him.

Couldn't have that.

Nick smiled his best I'm-just-an-ordinary-boring-old-guy smile, his harmless-as-can-be look.

Darlene and the waitress didn't appear to be buying it.

Which meant Nick had to be more careful.

Which meant keeping his mind on his own business was a good idea.

Which shouldn't be *that* hard.

She was just a woman, after all.

Nick hadn't met a woman yet that he couldn't handle.

Kim sat there with her sisters, Kate and Kathie, as well as Jax's wife, Gwen, who was very much a sister now, feeling happy as could be, as if absolutely all was right with the world. She was home. She was surrounded by her family and she was in love.

"So…tell us everything!" Kate commanded.

"Well, it was like all of a sudden he was all I could see, you know?"

The three of them nodded in unison, happy, girl-talk looks on their faces.

She was the only one of the three who was still single, the only one who'd never been in love. She'd been afraid it might never happen to her and now that it had, it was like it filled her entire body, like she was overflowing with this silly, giddy, bubbly, happy feeling. Like she couldn't even contain it.

She was babbling, but she couldn't help it. She didn't even want to help it. She wanted the whole world to know! Especially her sisters.

"Everything on the ship just got a little crazy and then there he was, right in front of me. He didn't look scared at all. He didn't even look surprised. He just looked like whatever happened, he could handle it, you know?"

They all sighed appreciatively.

"Self-confidence is just soooo sexy in a man," Gwen said.

Kathie nodded. "There's just something about a man who can handle anything. One you know you can count on."

"Yes," Kim said.

More sighs all around.

They were a bunch of happy women. Syrupy, gooey, mushy happy. It was that bad. And that good.

"So what did he do? The pirates attacked and then what?" Kate asked.

"He pushed me down on the deck, out of the way, because they had guns and were firing at the ship! Can you believe it?"

"No," they all said.

"No one could believe it," Kim said. "I thought it was fireworks at first or maybe a kid's game. The crew had some great games for the kids. I kept expecting an army of five-year-olds with toy guns to come running at any minute, explaining the noise and the commotion. And then we heard the bullets bouncing off the metal of the ship and people started screaming. It was crazy."

"Were you really scared?" Gwen asked.

"I don't know. I guess so… I mean, I don't know if I even had time to be scared. I'd just started to believe that maybe I should be scared and then…there he was." She grinned widely. It was like her face should hurt already, from grinning so much. She was just so ridiculously happy. "He pushed me down onto the deck and told me to stay down, then he put his own body between me and the pirates, like no matter what, he wasn't going to let them hurt me. We were on the lowest deck, not far at all from the surface of the water, right out in the open. It was the main sun deck, so it was full of space for lounge chairs and things. There was just nowhere to go for cover and he wouldn't let me move anyway."

Heavy, heavy sighs.

"Wow," Kathie said. "I'm so glad he was there to take care of you."

"Me, too," Kim said.

What would she have done without him? Maybe gotten herself shot, that's what.

"He stayed with me the whole time, until the entire thing was over and told me to stay calm, that everything would be all right, that he'd take care of me. He was wonderful!"

Nick heard that and thought he was going to puke.

Wonderful!

Near as they could tell, her Mr. Wonderful was on board to help the pirates board the ship, if the attack had gone just a little better. If Nick and his crew hadn't been waiting for them. Then Mr. Wonderful would have used pretty Kim Cassidy as cover while he helped his friends board the ship.

Nick could just see her with a gun at her head, Mr. Wonderful's arms wrapped around her, not to shield her but to keep her from getting away while the coward used her body to protect him and the thugs he worked with.

She'd really have thought he was something then.

Let her try to tell herself she was in love with the jerk then!

Of course, she didn't know that, poor, silly, naive woman that she was.

Why were the gorgeous ones always so…senseless when it came to men?

He'd wanted to say stupid. He'd normally say stupid. How could women be so stupid?

But he thought she was a nice woman, and not just because she had a great body, so he couldn't bring himself to call her stupid. He was already worrying about how she was going to take it when her lover boy turned out to be a crook.

He hoped he wouldn't have to be the one to tell her, but since it was his case, he'd probably have to do the deed.

She'd probably slap him. She'd cry. She might squeal, a really unhappy, awful squeal that wouldn't make him think of anything like taking her to bed with him. Not that she'd be getting anywhere near him once she knew what he was doing here.

Still, he didn't want her to cry.

He just wanted her to be smart and not get involved with jerks or pirates or international terrorists.

Was that too much to ask?

Nick watched, waited and listened as best he could as Kim chattered on.

He couldn't be sure, but he thought she'd said her new boyfriend was coming here…soon? Somebody had squealed again at that point in the conversation, so he just wasn't sure.

Maybe she'd call someone tonight and they'd have the phone tap in place and no one would squeal. Did women squeal on the phone, too? He hoped not. It was starting to make his head hurt.

Nick had finished his meal and the lunch rush was in full force. He ordered dessert to have an excuse to stay. It seemed half the town was there and that all of them knew Kim Cassidy and wanted to know about her adventure with the pirates. They all stopped at her table. She hugged quite a few of them, grinned broadly at others and gave them all a condensed version of the story.

Nick became aware that everyone in the place seemed to be talking about her.

He kept catching bits and pieces, none of which made sense.

"Engaged—" That from the guy in mechanic's overalls, heading to the cash register to pay his ticket.

Were they engaged? Surely not. Surely she wasn't that stupid.

Nick fought the urge to close his eyes and swear.

"From Colorado—"

So, the guy was from Colorado? That was something they could check. Nick made a mental note to tell Harry. *Check Colorado.*

"Cleveland—"

The guy in the dark blue suit said Cleveland?

Okay, check Colorado and Cleveland.

"Pittsburgh—"

What the hell? How could three different people in the same diner at the same time as her all think the guy was from three different places?

"Next week maybe—"

This from one of the waitresses who'd just been at Kim's table.

That was promising.

"Next month—"

No, no. Not next month. He would not make it until next month. Not here. Not with her.

"Huge party for them—"

"Soon as he gets here—"

"Falls Park—"

"Hold the crowd—"

"Award—"

Someone wanted to give the damned guy an award? For saving Kim?

Nick groaned.

"Great idea—"

"Talk to the mayor—"

"Talk to her sisters—"

"Award and engagement party, all at once—"

Nick hoped his head didn't explode and that he didn't blurt out something outrageous, like the truth of the matter, to everyone present at the Corner Diner that day.

Couldn't any of them get their stories straight?

Wasn't there one, solid, reliable piece of information in the whole place?

Other than the possibility that she might be engaged to the criminal?

Surely not.

Surely she wasn't that stupid.

He was thinking it now. Maybe the woman was just stupid. Nice but not very smart. From his experience, a frighteningly large number of women fit into that category. Maybe it wasn't their fault. Maybe they couldn't help it. Maybe men like Eric Weyzinski had some strange power over them and they just couldn't tell a jerk from a nice guy.

God knows Nick fooled enough of them into thinking everything he said was genuine, when hardly anything that came out of his mouth was.

Which, he realized, meant he had a lot in common with the crook who was about to break her heart.

"I don't know what to make of it," he told Harry once he got back to the B&B.

Kim had walked.

Nick had followed her very, very slowly.

Watched her stroll along like a woman without a care in the

world, smiling, stopping to talk to a dozen people along the way, staring up at the blue sky, stopping to smell the flowers.

It was like something out of one of those sickening long-distance commercials.

They were all so happy.

Nick didn't know what to make of it.

"What's the problem?" Harry said agreeably.

He said everything in that same I'm-your-buddy tone and it wasn't natural to be that happy. Nick tended to be suspicious of happy people. Harry and Kim and most people in this town were way too happy.

"I have no idea what's going on. That's the problem," Nick said, deciding to ignore the too-much-happiness thing for the moment. He had other more pressing concerns.

"You didn't hear anything at the diner?" Harry asked.

"No, I heard everything at the diner. That she might be engaged. That the guy was coming here, either the next day, the next week or the next month. Take your pick. That he's from Colorado or Cleveland or maybe Pittsburgh. What the hell?"

Harry laughed.

It was starting to annoy Nick every time Harry made that sound and Harry made it quite often.

"It's a small town," Harry said.

"So?"

"So people talk. All of them talk. All the time. But only about twenty percent of it's true, and that's just a guess. It might be less than twenty percent. I don't know. I don't think anybody knows."

"If I didn't know better, I'd say they were trying to confuse me," Nick said. "That all of them are in on it and they're deliberately trying to confuse me."

"No, they're just talking. They gossip. All about each other. Trust me, this is normal."

"Then how the hell am I supposed to figure out what's going on?"

"You follow her, Nickie. You stay really close to her. So close you can smell her pretty perfume. And you don't trust anything except what comes out of her sweet, little mouth and maybe not even that. Meanwhile, I'll look for your guy in Colorado, Cleveland and Pittsburgh. Who knows? Maybe we'll get lucky, and the guy'll show up tomorrow."

"Or maybe we won't."

"Yeah. Maybe." Harry chuckled. "Hey, I got the blueprint from the conversion they did on her house, when they cut it up into apartments. Am I crazy or is your view even more spectacular than we thought it might be?"

Nick said nothing.

"I mean, I don't have the same vantage point as you. But looking at it from street level, I'd have to say the angle is highly favorable. You could look into her living room and, off to the right, see through the doorway into her bedroom—"

"Shut up, Harry."

"You know you don't deserve perks like this, right? No man could be that lucky—"

Nick cut him off again.

He had hours before it got dark. Before she turned on the lights in her apartment and closed the blinds a little more tightly.

Would she do that? Or would she think she was far enough off the ground that no one could see in?

Maybe she wouldn't bother. After all, glancing around, he thought his was the only window with the perfect vantage point to be spying on her this way and if the B&B had been empty for some time while it was being renovated... Well, she might not have worried about anyone looking in on her.

Please let her close the blinds, he thought.

And please don't let her be in love with a crook who was going to break her heart.

Chapter Four

She made a few phone calls while sitting on the floor of her apartment doing some stretching moves that looked like yoga. Nick knew because he watched her every move. He sat on the floor, leaning against the wall, looking down into her apartment from what was, as Harry guessed, a perfect vantage point and watched nothing but her for hours.

She had the light on, as light was fading outside, and he kept his light off, his window blinds angled downward, his own private pipeline to her living room and tiny kitchen and, off to the right—yes, indeed—was the open door to her bedroom and bathroom. Not a great view into those rooms, but a view.

Nick listened in on the calls as she made them.

Two friends from high school, another from college. Fellow teachers at the elementary school where classes had ended only two weeks before. All wanting to know the same thing—what had happened on her trip?

Was he mistaken or did she sound less excited with each recitation of events? Did she sound a little sad? Maybe a little worried?

He thought she did.

And he had a name the guy had given her.

Eric Daniels.

An occupation. Something vague having to do with investments.

Yeah, right.

The place? Apparently, the guy moved around a lot because she did indeed mention the guy being in Colorado and Cleveland. No Pittsburgh. And apparently, his home base was California. She didn't mention a city. So half of what Nick had heard at the diner had some basis in reality? How was he supposed to function in this town?

She vacuumed and dusted her apartment, and he watched. She cleaned out the refrigerator and wiped down the countertops, and he watched. She went into the bathroom and, judging from the time she spent in there and the way she looked when she came out, she must have taken a bath. Nick, thankfully, saw nothing but the closed bathroom door and a view of her that made him groan out loud when she emerged, hair wrapped in a towel with a few damp curls escaping down her pretty neck, a flimsy, shimmering robe—God help him—clinging to what had to be still slightly damp curves, bare legs peeking out from the slit in the ends when she walked. Bare feet, he thought. Bare toes. With his high-powered binoculars, which he'd gotten out and used out of sheer curiosity, he caught a hint of bold color on her toenails and felt like a complete voyeur.

Which he was.

He was a damned Peeping Tom.

Night had fallen.

Her living room was lit with the light of a lamp in the corner. She had window blinds, but they were angled up toward the sun, no doubt to let the light in. But Nick was sitting there by his window, maybe five feet higher than hers, and he could see everything.

It looked like she was talking to herself, humming or maybe singing—some silly song about being in love, he feared.

He watched the robe billow out and flow behind her as she walked, the fabric swishing slightly this way and that with the movement of her hips. She grabbed a bottle of lotion out of the bathroom, propped her leg up on the coffee table in the living room and started smoothing it down her legs and onto her feet. That was…okay. He could handle that. He'd seen her put on sunscreen lotion on the ship and survived to tell the tale.

Then her hands started working their way up, slipping under the ends of the robe, to her pretty thighs. Had to keep that tan looking good, he suspected, groaning as he watched her hands move over herself. It was so much worse than what he'd seen on the ship. Her out-in-public touching herself had been difficult enough, but her alone-in-her-nightclothes touching herself was something out of an erotic film. She hadn't really looked up at him and said, *Do you want to touch me here?* Had she?

No. She hadn't.

It was just all too easy to imagine that she had, imagine his hands following hers.

They could play a game.

His hands following hers, wherever they went, wherever she wanted.

Nick made a pitiful, whimpering sound.

Honest to God, he was pathetic.

She pushed up a sleeve and spread lotion over one of her forearms and then the other.

Okay. That was better.

Then one of her hands slipped inside her robe, working on her neck, her shoulder and, he suspected, her chest.

Nick decided it was one of the sexiest things he'd ever seen. Pretty Kim Cassidy rubbing lotion all over herself, her hands slipping beneath her own robe, caressing her own bare skin.

You're going straight to hell for this one day, Nick told himself.

Straight to hell.

What was it about a woman touching herself that did this to men?

He'd never understood it, never bought it.

The man should want to be the one doing the touching, right? Not the other way around.

His hands on her. That's what a man should want.

But with her he got the whole fantasy thing.

Got that silly male voyeur thing and the effect of her with her hands all over her body and what it was doing to him. It was like an invitation, he decided. He could imagine her whispering, *See what I'm doing? Come here. You could be doing this, too.*

Or she could simply be giving him some helpful hints. *See this? I like this. I like to be touched like this.*

Fine by him.

He had a raging hard-on and couldn't take his eyes off her.

He imagined her getting ready for a date to show up. For a lover. Soaking in her bath, the water a little murky, just enough to keep him from having a perfectly clear view of her. Her hair would be piled on her head, her face and arms damp with moisture from the heat and the bath. Her eyes would be closed, dreamily, her knees breaking the surface of the water as she hunched down in the tub and maybe the tips of her breasts visible, too. She'd lie there, sweet perfume in the water seeping into every inch of her skin, and then she'd get out, water running down her body in ways that made him groan. She'd towel herself off or maybe he'd dry her. She'd slip into that silky robe and maybe he'd watch while she rubbed lotion all over herself, getting herself ready. For him.

She'd smile when he showed up at the door, greet him wearing nothing but the robe and hold out her welcoming arms to him. He'd pull her to him, feeling every bit of the heat of her and her pretty curves through the thin silk of the robe, then slip his hands inside, as he'd just watched her do, running his hands over soft, silky, still-damp skin.

She'd open herself up to him in every way.

Would he carry her to the bedroom or stop at the couch, too impatient to go any farther? Or have her right there against the wall, that robe still wrapped around her, but pushed aside so he could see her breasts, her pretty thighs? He wasn't sure if he'd have the patience to take it off of her. To do anything more than he absolutely had to do to get where he wanted to be, which was inside of her.

He could just imagine what she'd feel like in his arms, how she'd taste, the little sounds she'd make as…

As…

The lights went out.

Nick blinked once, then again.

He couldn't see anything anymore.

No more Kim in her pretty robe, her hands all over herself.

She'd turned out the light!

And left him sitting here practically panting after her, having some damned sexual fantasy worthy of a seventeen-year-old Peeping Tom.

Nick groaned, a mixture of disgust at himself and frustrated desire. Completely inappropriate for a man in his position but, honestly, he was just a man and she'd been… Well, she'd been doing things any woman might do in the privacy of her own apartment. In what she believed was the privacy of her own apartment.

How many women expected someone like Nick to be watching their every semierotic move while in the privacy of their own apartment?

Nick fought the urge to beat his own head against the wall.

Women who fell in love with crooks and potential terrorists should expect exactly this sort of treatment and should exercise some caution all around. He wanted to go give her a lecture on the subject, to yell at her until she listened to him and understood and promised to be more careful in the future. He wanted to tell her she didn't love that jerk, that he was nothing but a manipulating bastard, far more experienced in using people than she would ever be, and that she shouldn't feel too bad about this. It was just a simple mistake that innocent women like her made all too often.

He was fairly certain she was innocent in all this. Way too trusting and falling in love too easily and just not taking the kind of care with her emotions that she should take.

Of course, he couldn't tell her any of that. She couldn't even know he was watching.

And he had to keep doing this, night after night, just like this.

Did she take a bath every night? he wondered.

Did she always wear the robe and put lotion on herself like that?

He was doomed, Nick decided.

Doomed.

* * *

Kim got up early, ate an apple, talked to her sister Kate on the phone, then dressed in a little T-shirt, shorts and sandals.

She planned to take a walk to the nearby Falls Park to check out the fountain she was redoing as a summer art project with some of the kids from Big Brothers Big Sisters. But as she left her apartment, she happened to glance over at Mrs. Baker's and there, sitting on the patio all by himself, was Nick Cavanaugh, not moving at all, not even… Was he even awake?

Kim waited, standing just on the other side of the low hedge that separated Mrs. Baker's property from Kim's landlady's.

He was so still she wasn't even sure he was breathing. He sat in one of the big, comfy, cushioned Adirondack chairs, his head leaning against the back of it, a dark pair of sunglasses on and… No, wait… Every now and then she could see his chest rise and fall, so he was breathing at least. Deeply and slowly. She knew because she watched.

Just to the right of where he sat, a curtain in the window was pushed aside. Mrs. Baker looked out, saw Kim, then motioned for her to wait; Mrs. Baker was coming out.

She stopped opposite Kim, on the other side of the hedge, stared back at Nick, shook her head and whispered, "Poor man. I don't think he's well."

"Really?"

Mrs. Baker nodded. "I was stripping wallpaper in the dining room until all hours and I was being quiet because that room is right below his bedroom. He kept getting up, walking around, going back to bed. Getting up, walking around, going back to bed. Couldn't sleep at all. I went to the door and knocked, asked him if he was all right and he swore that he was, but I'm not so sure. He practically begged for a room here. Said he'd been up all night on an overnight flight from South America, hadn't gotten any rest and had a bad back, I think. Or maybe his shoulder. He seems to be favoring both. And he was limping, too. When he couldn't sleep I wondered if he was in pain or something. And for him to be sleeping outside this morning… I thought the poor man must be simply exhausted when he first came, but now I'm worried it might be something more. Something serious."

"He wouldn't tell you what was wrong last night?" Kim asked.

"No. Not a word. Do you think he's all right over there? I mean, he's just sleeping, right? I don't want my first official guest collapsing here or well…you know? I can't lose my first guest. That would be a terrible omen."

Kim frowned.

Mrs. Baker tended to worry too much and Kim didn't think Nick Cavanaugh was dying. Granted, there was something a little off about him and he seemed tired yesterday and a little bit… Not grumpy. Rattled? Distracted? Easily confused? No, not that. Just…off.

But she liked Mrs. Baker a lot and the woman put a lot of stock in her omens and little twinges and all sorts of things like that.

"Would you go make sure he's okay?" Mrs. Baker asked. "I'd do it myself, but I don't think he appreciated my concern when I asked him last night. It was like I'd caught him doing something he shouldn't or… Well, that's the way it felt to me."

"Okay. I'll talk to him," Kim said.

"I'll bring you two some tea, to give you an excuse to sit and talk awhile."

Mrs. Baker went inside to make tea. Kim walked around the hedges and onto Mrs. Baker's patio, pausing there, trying to decide what to do. She didn't want to startle him. If he had been up all night in pain, he probably needed his rest this morning. And it wasn't like the man wasn't breathing.

Kim sat down in the chair next to his, leaned back and propped her feet up on the comfy stool in front of her chair to wait. If he wasn't awake when Mrs. Baker came out with their tea, she'd wake him up. Until then, it was a gorgeous, early-summer morning. The sky was a happy shade of light blue, the sun was beaming down on them. There was a perfect, slight breeze and the temperatures hadn't yet climbed too high.

She could almost imagine she was back on the ship, before the pirates hit, when she hadn't had a care in the world.

Kim leaned back and closed her eyes, picturing Eric's handsome face, trying not to worry that she hadn't heard from him.

She'd been sure he'd call last night but he hadn't, and she hadn't been able to reach him at the number he gave her. Oh, he could have been stuck on a plane somewhere and gotten in really late, especially considering the time difference on the West Coast. That was probably it. Surely he'd call today.

She couldn't wait for him to get here, to meet her family, to see her hometown, just to be here with her.

Love was intoxicating, she decided. Overwhelming. Addictive. She couldn't stop thinking about him, missing him, dreaming about him. She was sure she had a silly grin on her face and didn't even care. He was wonderful. He was amazing. He was her dream man come to life and she didn't care how silly that sounded, either. It was true.

She sighed, stretching her arms above her head and sinking more deeply into the cushions of her chair. At the edge of the stone patio, Mrs. Baker's cat, a giant black-and-white fur ball named Cleo, ambled ever so slowly toward Kim. Kim held out a hand to Cleo, expecting the cat to jump into her lap so she could pet it.

But no. Cleo ignored her completely and went to sniff at Nick's left leg instead.

"Cleo, no," Kim whispered. "He's tired. Poor guy. He didn't sleep well."

But Cleo couldn't imagine anyone not wanting to meet her or fuss over her. Shy, she was not.

Before Kim could stop her, the cat jumped up into Nick's lap.

He came awake in a flash with a menacing-sounding growl.

Nick, not the cat, growling.

His hand was at his left side in a flash, searching but unable to find the cat.

That was odd.

Cleo weighed twenty pounds if she weighed an ounce. How hard could it be to find her on someone's lap?

Kim watched as Nick's right hand fumbled around on his side, near his left shoulder, while the cat stood up on all fours, back arched, hissing in Nick's face.

"What the hell?" Nick said, pulling off his sunglasses and throwing them down, breathing hard and staring down at the startled cat.

"Rrrrraaarrrr!" the cat howled.

Kim could practically see the cat's claws sinking into Nick's lap in what had to be truly unfortunate places.

Ouch.

"It's okay. It's just the cat," she said.

He looked over at her with the same kind of expression he'd used upon finding the cat in his lap, like he couldn't quite believe she was that close to him and he hadn't known it. Like he didn't quite know where he was or didn't believe what his own eyes were telling him.

Had he been drinking or something? Maybe taking some pain medication for his shoulder?

Kim looked at him with genuine concern.

He scowled back at her.

"Are you all right?" she asked.

"No, I am not all right," he said, enunciating each word carefully and distinctly, like he didn't quite trust his own powers of speech. "What the hell is going on?"

"You fell asleep," she said, using her best calm-down-the-panicking-kindergarteners voice on him, because he looked about as freaked out as those kids did on the first day of school when their mommies left. "You're on the patio at Mrs. Baker's house. Remember?"

He looked like he thought she was spinning lies that he wasn't about to buy, but then did a slow, careful study of the backyard, ending up with his gaze locked with Cleo's, his expression one of a man who might never have seen a cat before.

Cleo, for her part, gave him a regal stare, as if he were a peasant ignoring the needs of his queen, who was ready to be fussed over. The arch came slowly out of her back. Kim thought the cat sheathed her claws, hoped so for Nick's sake. Cleo tiptoed around in a circle on his lap, picking her spot ever so carefully, then settled down against him once more and waited, looking at him as if he might be a complete imbecile.

"Rrrraaarrrr," she said demandingly, then proceeded to wriggle around until she was lying on her back, paws curled up in the air, presenting him with her huge, furry belly.

Nick looked even more insulted than the cat.

"She just wants you to pet her," Kim said.

"Yeah, well I want a lot of things that I don't think I'm going to get today."

But his hand settled carefully along the cat's belly just the same.

He didn't seem to have any trouble controlling his hand now, Kim noted.

How odd.

What had he been doing before?

He didn't pet the cat. It was more a hand to hold the cat in place, Kim decided.

Cleo once again shot him her you-can't-possibly-be-that-stupid, you-must-know-exactly-what-I-expect look.

It did no good.

Nick looked over at Kim, like a man trying to figure out how he came to be in this place, how she came to be beside him and what might have gone on before the cat jumped in his lap.

"You fell asleep," she said again. "Remember?"

"That's impossible," he claimed.

"Why? You don't sleep?"

"Not in a public place," he claimed.

So...he had a phobia about sleeping in public?

"Then you were just relaxing with your eyes closed for quite a while," she said, again as she might explain to a five-year-old. You just couldn't argue with some people. In these cases she tended to simply state her position and move on. She wasn't that invested in when or where the man slept, so she was more amused than anything else by his whole attitude.

Mrs. Baker would just be glad he wasn't dead.

Cleo gave another little roar and wriggled around into a more comfortable position. She was clearly not pleased about the lack of attention being shown her.

"*It* sank its claws into me," Nick said.

"Well, you startled her."

"I think she's clearly the one who startled me," he said.

"Well, maybe she thought you were just relaxing with your eyes closed, not sleeping. Maybe she knows you don't sleep in public, so she thought it was perfectly safe to jump up there and not have to worry about pulling you abruptly out of sound sleep and startling you," Kim reasoned.

Nick looked even more annoyed.

She fought the urge to laugh. He was just out of sorts, but his confusion was so complete and seemed so genuine, she found it amusing. He didn't seem like a man who was often confused or caught so unaware.

"Her name is Cleo. She's Mrs. Baker's. I'm surprised she hasn't granted you an audience before now. She usually can't wait for everyone to admire her."

Cleo purred contentedly now that she'd found her spot snuggled into the furrow of his thighs.

"No claws," Nick ordered.

"You might as well just pet her. She won't leave until you do and I'm betting she's more stubborn than you," Kim told him.

"You think I'm going to be held hostage by a cat?"

Kim just laughed.

For some reason the sights and sounds of Nick Cavanaugh annoyed, amused her.

"Did you need something?" he asked, as if he were still trying to figure things out.

"Actually, I just came to make sure you weren't dying."

Oh, that thoroughly confused him.

Kim could tell.

And found herself enjoying the moment even more.

He looked once again like he had when he'd been startled into consciousness by the cat.

"You wouldn't happen to be one of those people who are addicted to coffee, would you?" she tried.

"What?"

"One of those people who simply can't function without a few cups first thing in the morning? The kind of person you don't even want to speak to until they've had a hit of caffeine?"

"What are you talking about?"

"I mean, I know you didn't sleep well, but surely—"

"What do you know about how I slept?" he barked at her.

Okay, time for the soothe-the-five-year-old thing again. "Mrs. Baker said you didn't sleep well—"

"She talks to you about her guests' sleeping habits?" he asked incredulously.

"She was concerned. She heard you up pacing all night and then with you complaining about being ill—"

"I am not ill," he said, doing that enunciate-every-word-with-a-hard-and-distinct-beat thing again.

"You told her you were when you begged her for a room. She told me so—"

"So she does tell you everything about her guests?"

"No. She was worried. She was afraid you weren't just asleep out here. That you'd collapsed or something."

His mouth opened, but no words came out.

Kim couldn't tell if he was more insulted or furious.

She fought to hold back a huge grin and added, "She just didn't want you dying in your sleep back here and no one noticing."

He cocked his head to the right, as if he might hear the words differently with his head at a different angle.

Kim giggled. She couldn't help it. "It would be a bad omen if her first guest died and she's big on omens and signs and things."

"So this is all about some weird superstition she has for the inn?"

"No. She's concerned about you, too. She's a nice lady."

"I. Am. Not. Dying," he said rather loudly.

Cleo got up on all fours, gave him her highly indignant look, jumped onto the patio and ran into the bushes.

"Sorry," Kim said.

"Do I look like a man who's dying?"

"No. I didn't say that—"

"I'm thirty-eight years old, for God's sake. I'm not dying!"

"Okay. Sorry—"

"I may be aching in a few places, sore in a few others." He rubbed at his right shoulder as he said it. "But I am not falling apart. Not yet."

"Okay. Good."

His hand fell to his side, no difficulties controlling it that Kim could see, and she felt bad now about enjoying his little temper tantrum so much. She put her hand on his shoulder, because touch could have a powerful calming effect. She used that with the kindergarteners, too.

His shoulder muscles were in knots. She rubbed her thumb lightly along the tightness there.

He threw her a look once again like he'd just been jerked out of a sound sleep.

Did the man have trouble waking up?

Maybe it was some kind of superstrong pain reliever whose effect hadn't yet worn off.

"You poor thing," she said. "What did you do to yourself?"

He was looking down at her hand on his shoulder like he had trouble believing she was touching him.

Drugs, she decided. Had to be.

He must be in so much pain.

"I fell down," he said. The kindergartener words coming out of a big, tall, grown-up man struck her as funny once again. A fall didn't seem like enough to do lasting damage to a grown man.

"Okay," Kim said, determined not to laugh once more. He'd looked so insulted when she'd done that before. "A long way down?"

"No. I just had help getting there."

Kim nodded. "You got into a fight?" Bloody nose? Grass-stained pants? Boys will be boys?

"Not exactly," he said, fountain of information that he was.

His muscles tensed even more under her light touch.

So, he'd fallen down and gotten a boo-boo? And she supposed there'd been no one around to kiss it and make it better.

Because he seemed to be a man in desperate need of soothing and some serious caretaking.

"Well, then…it's good that you came here to rest," she said.

He rolled his eyes and made a sound of disgust, turned his head to the side and swore softly under his breath. "You really think I'm falling apart?"

"No. Just that you're hurt, and I'm betting that you don't often get to slow down and rest. That you're not happy about it."

"No, I am not happy," he said, agreeing with her for once.

"Well, we'll try to make the time you spend here as pleasant and relaxing as possible," she said, getting to her feet.

"Thank you," he said, still looking all out of sorts.

What an odd man.

Mrs. Baker picked that moment to push open the door and walk onto the patio with a tea tray, an overly bright smile on her face, as if she knew already that things were not going well on the patio, that her guest found her concern an annoyance at best, more likely an out-and-out insult.

Mrs. Baker shot Kim a panicked look.

Kim shook her head. *No, it had not gone well. No, do not ask how he's feeling. Do not hover. Do not offer any sympathy.*

She tried to convey all of that with just a look and must have done well, because Mrs. Baker now seemed panicked about what to do.

Kim took the tray and sat it on a small table at Nick's side.

"Thank you so much," Kim said. "I have to run, but I bet Nick would really enjoy some nice, quiet time on the patio with his morning tea."

"Of course." Mrs. Baker shot her a grateful look and practically ran back inside.

"Thank you," Nick said when she was gone.

He was rubbing at his head, as if that hurt, too, now.

The poor man really was falling apart completely, no matter what he said.

"No problem," she said, staying on her feet, ready to make her escape, too.

"You're leaving?" he asked.

She nodded. "Try not to grumble at Mrs. Baker. She's nervous about opening the inn and she cries easily when she's nervous."

"I'll do my best not to drive her to tears," he said dryly.

That was it.

Kim escaped, shaking her head, puzzling over him.

What a truly odd man.

Chapter Five

With both of them gone, Nick could hear nothing but Harry laughing hilariously in his ear.

Laughing like there was no tomorrow.

Like if the world came to an end in that moment, Harry could die a happy man.

Nick swore long and loud, then turned around in his chair to make sure Mrs. Baker wasn't spying on him.

The woman was a damned snoop.

She'd hovered outside his door last night after she'd caught him pacing. He was sure of it. He had a sixth sense about these things and, besides, he heard her breathing out there.

"Dammit, Harry," he said. "You let me fall asleep out here and didn't say one damned word?"

"I figured you needed the rest," Harry said, still chuckling. "Hard night, Nickie?"

Pun intended, Nick was sure.

"Shut up, Harry."

"Great view, huh? I knew it."

"Harry, I swear to God, before this is over, I'm going to strangle you—"

"I heard she took a bath last night."

From Nick's own notes, no doubt, which Harry would have seen when he came on duty this morning.

Not only did Nick have to watch her, he had to write up a report on what he'd seen and e-mail it to Harry.

Not how much of her skin he'd seen or the way her own hands had run over her luscious body. Not that he needed a report to remember that.

"So...what does she wear when she gets out of her bath, Nick? Come on. Tell me. I can take it."

Nick just growled.

"Those little baby-doll pajama things? I just love those. I put ten bucks on those—"

"You're betting on what she sleeps in?"

"Yeah. It's kind of boring here. I don't have the view you do. What does she wear?"

"You have the mind of a thirteen-year-old boy. You know that, don't you?"

Harry laughed again. "And you don't? You weren't wondering what she'd be wearing when she tucked herself in? You weren't enjoying the view? You are one lucky son of a bitch, you know that, don't you, Nickie?"

"Yeah, I know it," Nick said.

He was lucky she hadn't given him a heart attack last night.

Did men his age have heart attacks?

He thought they might, in cases of extreme stress or maybe if they had some rare genetic disorder.

Nick wasn't sure his heart was tough enough to make it

through this assignment. He was still sweating just thinking of her coming out of the bath last night and he hadn't slept a damned bit for thinking of it, either.

Which meant it was no surprise that he'd fallen asleep out here this morning.

Except now she thought he was some kind of cripple. An invalid. A man in danger of dropping dead on Mrs. Baker's patio.

Nick swore once again.

"How old do I look to you, Harry?"

Harry started laughing, again, so hard that he couldn't talk.

"Oh, hell, never mind," Nick said.

"No, no, no. I understand, believe me. We all hit that age."

Nick was afraid to ask, but forced himself to. "What age?"

"The invisible-to-women age."

"Harry, she saw me. She might think I'm falling apart, but she definitely saw me."

"No, I mean as a man. You know. Someone they check out automatically to see if they're interested. We all hit a certain age where women, attractive women of a certain age, just don't notice us anymore in that way. They might see us, but they don't see us. You know?"

Oh, hell. Nick was afraid he did.

He was staring and panting after a woman who saw him as nothing but a non-man? An un-man? An old man!

Nick swore long and loud.

She did. She saw him as nothing but someone who might croak on her next-door-neighbor's patio, bringing on all sorts of bad luck or bad omens or something like that. But nothing of him as a man, except as a broken-down one.

"Yeah, it hurts, doesn't it?" Harry said. "Especially with a looker like her."

"She's twenty-four, Harry," Nick said, trying to salvage what he could of his pride. "Men our age running around with twenty-four-year-olds look ridiculous, you know?"

"Hell, do you think I'd care how it looked to anyone else, if she'd have me? You think I'd be worried about how anybody but her looked, under those circumstances?"

Okay, Harry had a point.

A good point.

But not one Nick wanted to hear at the moment.

"Just tell me where she went, okay?"

They had to get somewhere on this investigation. So they could wrap it up and get out of here. So Nick didn't have to watch her apartment while she took her bath and while she walked out of the bathroom after taking her bath, wrapped up in nothing but that robe, and then while she rubbed lotion all over herself, looking like a male fantasy come to life.

He had to get out of here.

She went to the park, five blocks away.

Harry laughed when Nick got in his car and drove. To get there faster, Nick claimed. Harry laughed when Nick flinched as he climbed into the tiny convertible, the midlife-crisis mobile, as Harry had taken to calling it. Perfect for Nick, of course. He laughed as Nick tried unsuccessfully not to limp on his bad knee walking down the path into the park.

It was the slope, Nick told himself. It put more pressure on the knee than he needed right now. And he'd slept funny, when he'd slept, and woken up with the knee throbbing.

Yeah, that was his excuse and he was sticking to it.

When this was over, he was never working with Harry again.

Nick tried not to grimace as he spotted her, standing by a big, round fountain in the middle of the park. She was juggling a notebook, a pen and a tape measure, not too successfully, frowning as she tried to jot something down.

The sun was shining overhead, bright and way too cheery, as far as Nick was concerned. His head hurt. His knee hurt. And he had to talk to her without scowling, without sending her scrambling to get away from him and, hopefully, without picturing her in her robe, her hands running over the bare skin underneath it.

He scowled once again.

"Scary, Nick," Harry said into his ear. "Scary, scary. Remember, don't want to scare her."

Harry was a magician. He was everywhere at once. All-seeing, all-knowing. And annoying as hell.

Nick hit a button, releasing him from the link that piped Harry directly into his head.

Little Miss I'm-In-Love-With-A-Terrorist chose that moment to look up from the notebook she'd been scribbling in to see Nick and frown.

It was quick, gone almost before it began, but Nick saw it and couldn't blame her for it. He didn't really want to be anywhere near himself, either, not in this mood.

Unfortunately, nobody asked him what he wanted to do today.

He was stuck with her.

He smiled. He could do that when it was absolutely necessary.

"Small world, huh?" he tried.

She frowned up at him. "Are you following me or something?"

"Who?" Nick looked around, feigning innocence as best he could. It wasn't his best emotion, but he thought he could do a reasonable facsimile when absolutely necessary. "Me?"

"Yes, you. You're the only one here. You and I are the only ones here."

"No. I…I…" He looked around for some kind of answer and his gaze landed on a sign that said Magnolia Falls with an arrow pointing off to the right. "I came to look at the falls."

Were there falls?

He hoped so, vaguely remembered something about them in the briefing report he'd read last night. The one he was supposed to have been studying while he made like a Peeping Tom staring into her window.

She put her hand on her hips and cocked her head to the side, beautiful blond hair catching the light as she did so.

"You came to look at the falls?"

"Yes. I like…waterfalls. I mean…who doesn't like waterfalls?"

She looked at him like he might be the kind to enjoy tearing the wings off butterflies or something equally sadistic. Crossing her arms in front of her, she said, "With your bad knee, bad back and bad shoulder, you decided to take a hike this morning?"

Nick, all but on death's doorstep, gritted his teeth, imagining Mrs. Baker gossiping about his litany of health issues with a superbly-shaped twenty-four-year-old. "My doctor said exercise was a good idea for the knee."

As if a stroll in the damned park was something he'd ever consider exercise.

She obviously thought it would be to a broken-down, old man like him. Because she accepted his explanation right away.

"Oh. Well, they're just past that clump of trees, but it's about a mile from here. If you'd parked on the other side of the park, you would have only been about fifty feet away from one of the nicest views of the falls."

Nick nodded. "Must have gotten turned around on my directions."

Now she could think he was feebleminded as well as feeble-bodied.

Great.

"Look, I'm sorry about this morning," he said. "You just startled me. You and the cat. And I didn't get a lot of sleep last night, but that's no excuse. I shouldn't have taken my bad mood out on you."

"Is that an apology?" she asked.

He hesitated, not sure of the right answer. "Yes?"

She laughed.

Nick frowned. "The apology needs work, too?"

"No. It's fine. You just reminded me of someone. One of my students."

She looked like she made a fine private joke, but Nick knew—she taught elementary school kids.

He reminded her of a little kid? Worse, a little kid in a snit?

And he couldn't even let her know that he knew she was insulting him.

"I remind you of someone who annoys you?" he said, trying not to sound too peeved. He had to try to get her to like him well enough to chitchat with him about the love of her life, the pirate, after all.

"And amuses me," she said, blinking up at him with eyes that were as clear-blue as the sky above their heads.

"Oh," he said.

What could he say?

She got to insult him if she wanted to, while he had to make nice to her and try not to think of her nearly naked. Annoying her would probably not help in that regard. He wondered if Harry had a parabolic mike on them and had picked up the entire conversation. Or if Harry read lips. Nick often suspected the man did. Or had some kind of mystical powers when it came to snooping. Harry knew way too much.

Nick feared he was scowling again.

Kim Cassidy was laughing.

"I'm sorry," she said. "You're just...well, you're a funny man."

"Funny as in strange?"

"Maybe. I don't know. I was thinking more amusing. I can't tell if you're being sarcastic all the time or just honest."

"I've been accused of having a pessimistic streak and a very dry sense of humor," Nick admitted.

Which amused her all the more.

"Yes. That!" she said. "Are you annoyed with me or just stating the obvious? I can't begin to tell."

Again, Nick had no idea what the right answer might be and he needed the right answer. He needed to stay here with her and find out what was going on with her and lover boy.

"I'm trying not to be... annoying," he said finally.

"Okay."

"It doesn't come easy to me some days."

She nodded. At least she wasn't laughing now. She was looking at him like she might feel sorry for him, which he liked even less but probably suited his purpose better.

What the hell was he supposed to say now?

"Nice fountain." It was all he could come up with.

She was standing by the thing, after all. Sketching it, from what he could see of the pad of paper in her hand.

"It's my summer project," she said, flipping through the sketchbook and then turning it to face him, showing him drawings of designs for the bottom of what looked like this fountain. "We're going to design and install a mosaic on the bottom and maybe on the sidewalk around the edges of the fountain."

"We?"

"Me and a bunch of teenagers who managed to flunk an introductory art class and were sentenced to summer school."

"They flunked an introductory art class?"

Kim nodded, a hand resting on the outside wall of the fountain, assessing it with a critical eye.

It was about fifteen feet in diameter, round and shallow, made of weathered concrete with something that looked like a cartoon fairy on top. Or maybe a mermaid. Who could tell? Nick wasn't exactly an art connoisseur.

"You can imagine, they're less than enthusiastic about being in class with me this summer," she said. "I thought being outside, having lots of mallets and being able to pound glass into little pieces might hold their attention, so I talked the city council and the school district into letting us redo the fountain."

Nick frowned, couldn't help it. "Are any of them violent? Because being around them with mallets and broken glass—"

"They're kids who flunked art, not criminals," she claimed. "Okay…some of them might have been in a few minor skirmishes, but nothing serious."

"Define *nothing serious,*" he said.

"Now you sound like my brother."

"Good for him. You should listen to him."

She got a stubborn look on her face. An annoyed look. And damned if it wasn't adorable.

"If I listened to my brother, I'd never go anywhere and I'd never do anything—"

"Good for him," Nick said again, then knew this was as

good an opening as he was ever going to get. "Which reminds me, were you really attacked by pirates?"

"No. Not really," she claimed. "The ship I was on was attacked by pirates, but they didn't even get on board and they didn't get anywhere near me. Someone at the diner told you?"

He nodded. It was true. They had. They'd told him fifteen different stories about her and the pirates before he'd lost count of them and given up on remembering them, sure there wasn't the slightest bit of truth to any of them.

Which he realized could work for him now.

"Actually, they told me at least fifteen different versions of the story of you and the pirates," he admitted. "It was all very confusing and I'd swear most of their stories consisted of nothing but outlandish lies."

"Small-town living at it's best," she said.

"So do I get to hear the truth? From you? Because I figure there must be some shred of truth to it and, who knows, we might all need to be on the lookout for pirates one day?"

"You're making fun of me—"

"No. Really. I mean, if it happened to you, it could happen to anyone, right? I could get attacked by pirates tomorrow—"

"In Magnolia Falls, Georgia—"

"And I wouldn't know what to do. And you'd feel guilty about it," Nick said, for a moment forgetting himself and talking just for the sake of arguing with her, because, well, he liked it. "I mean, look how badly I handled being attacked by that vicious cat with the three-inch claws."

"Cleo doesn't have a vicious bone in her body. She's just overly friendly."

"And free and easy in applying her claws to my lap. There's no telling what kind of injuries I sustained."

"To go along with your bad shoulder, knee and back?"

"There is nothing wrong with my back," he said.

Did she really think he was old and falling apart? Not that he should care.

Or had he reached that hideous state Harry had described? Invisible to women of a certain age?

Nick cringed.

Not that he made a habit of chasing after women half—well, not exactly half his age—two-thirds his age?

No, she wasn't two-thirds his age.

Women between half and two-thirds of his age?

Which sounded every bit as pathetic as chasing after women half his age.

"You looked happy for just a moment," she said.

Nick shrugged. "What can I say? I have my moments."

"That's all? Moments of happiness."

At this point she looked as if she actually cared. Or maybe just felt sorry for him. Who could tell? And what did it matter anyway?

Nick was happy running around, chasing criminals, righting wrongs. He'd do that for as long as he could and when he couldn't anymore… Well, he'd worry about it when the time came.

He'd leave. Kim would be a little wiser, a little sadder, and life would go on. She'd find someone who wasn't a criminal and she'd be fine staying right here in her little town, listening to gossip at the diner and being looked after by her older brother, the cop, and fussed over by her sisters.

Nothing to worry about here.

"You know, since you're here, you could help me for a moment, if it's not too much trouble. I need to take some measurements of the fountain, so the class and I can make design plans." She held up a tape measure and waited.

She thought he couldn't handle holding on to one end of a tape measure?

What did she think? That he was going to collapse from standing up too long in the sun?

Oh, hell.

How bad did he look?

"I think I can manage," he said, hoping he didn't sound too sarcastic, too disgusted or too grumpy.

Must not have managed, because she sighed heavily. "I just thought....you know.... Leaning over the edge and into the water to measure the work space we have on the bottom of the fountain. I thought it might aggravate your knee or maybe your shoulder—"

"And since I am practically on death's door—"

"That's not what I said. Not at all. I was just concerned—"

"Give me the damned tape measure," he said, holding out his hand.

She plopped it down on his palm none too gently.

"Where to?"

"Right where you are is fine," she said.

So he didn't have to be troubled with moving, he realized, when she grabbed the end of the tape measure and pulled it along with herself as she walked to the other side of the fountain.

Harry must be about to bust a gut laughing, if he'd heard that.

Nick shook his head and tried not to scowl.

Scary Nick. Scary Nick.

No good for getting the woman to talk to him.

He obediently held his end of the tape measure as instructed. Inside the fountain and along its outer edge. Circumference, radius, every angle imaginable, while she took notes and made a diagram.

She was wading in the fountain in her short shorts, mapping out the base of the statue while Nick tried not to look at her legs, when a woman Nick would swear had to be a small-town librarian her entire life came along, giving him a thorough once-over.

"Kim, is this your young man?" she said, smiling up at Nick, who stood there with his tape measure trying for all the world not to look scary or grumpy.

At least she didn't think he was decrepit. So what if she was sixty if she was a day?

"Hi, Ms. Applebaum. How are you?"

"Fine, dear. And you?"

"Great."

"We're all so happy you're home safely."

"Me, too. This is my temporary neighbor, Nick Cavanaugh. He's Mrs. Baker's first guest at the B&B."

Nick took the hand she held out and shook it.

"Not Kim's young man?"

Nick shook his head. "Afraid not." And tried not to think about how he felt about being referred to as a *young man* by a sixty-year-old small-town librarian, as sexless a creature as he could imagine.

He was grateful, he feared.

Pathetically grateful.

"Well, welcome," Mrs. Applebaum said, then turned to Kim. "And your young man? When will he be joining us?"

"Any day now," Kim said.

"Well, good. We're all dying to meet the man who captured our Kimmie's heart."

Kim smiled, chitchatted, then said goodbye, but Nick didn't think she was all that happy.

They went back to taking measurements. She was very thorough and getting the measurements she wanted often involved her bending over and him trying not to watch the way her top gaped open just a bit, giving him a shadowy view of what he knew from his surveillance on the ship while she was sunbathing was a chest that would be considered a museum-quality work of art.

"Going to tell me about you and the pirates?" he said finally, trying to keep his mind on his job.

"There's not much to it," she said, straightening up, thank goodness. "I was nearly asleep on the pool deck when I heard shouting and what I thought were fireworks or something like that. Granted, it was daytime and thinking it was fireworks was not the smartest thing I could have done, which my brother has already explained to me in excruciating detail. He's a cop—"

Nick nodded.

"And instead of getting out of the way, because I thought it was fireworks I just sat there, looking for pretty colors and patterns in the sky and things like that." She finally climbed out of the fountain, sitting on the ledge and swinging a pair of perfect legs over the side. "Then I woke up a bit more and thought…kid's game? You know, with fake guns and things? Because real bullets were zinging by me by then. And then someone came along and saved me."

She got a kind of dreamy look on her face at the mention of her new man.

"Someone you're in love with, I heard," Nick said.

She grinned. "Yes."

"Which your brother isn't happy about?"

"Yes. That story's making the rounds, too?"

"I told you. Fifteen different stories. That was just one of the ones that sounded plausible, given what you've already said about your brother."

"So, that's really all there is to it. My great adventure with the pirates at sea."

"And now the whole town's waiting for a glimpse of your new man, right?" Nick said.

"Yes."

"And he's coming soon?"

She didn't look quite so happy then.

Damn.

Nick had been hoping it would happen fast, that he could escape, get her out of harm's way and be done with it before she had time to get hurt too badly.

Where the hell was the guy?

"What's wrong?" he asked.

She shrugged, hugging her sketchbook to her chest. "I haven't heard from him since I left the ship."

"Oh."

That was bad.

Very bad.

What if the guy didn't need her for anything else? What if he was just flirting with her, toying with her, making her fall in love with him for no reason at all, other than the fact that she was there and gorgeous and one of the sexiest women Nick had ever seen, with that innocent small-town-girl way of hers?

Maybe it was just that she looked so innocent that it made the seduction that much more fun to a rat like him.

Nick scowled. Couldn't help it.

"I'm sure everything's fine," Kim said, sounding like she was trying to convince herself as much as him.

"Sure. It's only been…" He almost tripped himself up. Damn. "How long has it been?"

"Thirty-seven hours since he walked me to my gate at the airport, then flew home himself."

Which meant she was counting every hour as it passed. "He's not answering his phone?"

She shook her head, looking that much sadder.

"Well, it could be anything," Nick reasoned. "Phone trouble. Plane trouble. He could have come back to a mess at work that accumulated in the time he was gone."

"I know."

Still, she was obviously not used to being ignored, especially by a man she was supposed to be madly in love with.

And what man in his right mind would ignore her?

Certainly not a sane one. Not an innocent one.

"You know, I've got a friend from college who works for the phone company. I could ask him to check out the number for you."

She brightened at that. "Really?"

Nick nodded, thinking, *Give me the number. Just give it to me.*

"He's done it for me before," Nick said. "When I wrote down a number wrong for a business contact. Stuff like that. It's nothing to him. Wouldn't take him five minutes, I bet."

"And he could tell us if the number's working?"

Nick nodded, thinking, *Don't be in love with this jerk. Please don't be in love with him.*

"Okay. That would be great. He lives in California," she said, then rattled off the number.

She'd memorized it. Because she'd been calling the jerk round the clock, Nick feared.

Because she was in love with a crook.

Chapter Six

He called Harry right then and there to relay the number.

"You dog, you," Harry said. "She just gave it to you?"

"That's right. Anything you can find out, my friend would appreciate."

"You two are friends now? That's sweet, Nickie. Really sweet. And I hear she's dripping wet again—"

"Harry—"

"Yeah, yeah. Okay. You still got it, Nick. Don't let anybody tell you that you don't, because you do."

"Yeah, I've got it."

He could lie to women with the best of 'em.

It was a real talent.

He hung up the phone, reassured the beautiful, dripping-wet woman who'd been wading in a fountain with him all morning that he would have some information for her very, very soon, then stood there by her fountain as she thanked him.

"No problem," he said, while trying to figure out what he'd tell her the next time he saw her about her would-be-terrorist/love-of-her-life.

While he tried to figure out what it would be to his advantage—and to his investigation's advantage—to tell her. Not what would be best for her. It couldn't be about her and getting her the hell away from this man and maybe keeping her from feeling any more foolish or hurt than she'd already be.

"You're scowling again," she said.

"Just thinking," he said, tucking his phone away.

"About?"

"A work problem."

"To do with the falls?"

He nodded.

"What kind of work do you do with a waterfall?"

"I'm a city planner." He made it up on the spot. "Working with a town in Pennsylvania. They're interested in having a park similar to this. I'm here to gather information about the park."

Which would give him an excuse to wander around, taking notes and things, while she and her juvenile delinquents played with mallets and broken glass if his assignment lasted that long. Yeah, that was what he was going to say if anyone asked what he was doing in town.

"You design parks?" Kim asked.

Nick nodded.

Her look said she had a hard time believing it.

"What? I like parks." Everyone liked parks, didn't they?

"You just don't seem like the park type."

"Well, there's a difference between designing them and wanting to hang out on the playground in one or climb a tree," he said, *Scary Nick* coming through loud and clear, he was sure.

"I guess so," Kim said.

"You probably still like to climb trees, right?" He was really trying not to be so grouchy.

"Are you actually attempting to make a joke?" she asked incredulously.

"I make jokes. I'm a funny guy."

She laughed hilariously at that.

He frowned.

"Okay, if I'm not all that funny, why do you keep laughing at me?"

She tried to tell him but she was laughing too hard to speak.

He wasn't sure whether to feel insulted or annoyed.

He didn't want to like her. It was bad enough that she was gorgeous and that her window was at a perfect angle for him to look inside her apartment at night. Feeling guilty about what he was doing here and how she was no doubt going to be hurt didn't help, either. But liking her—really liking her and thinking she was a nice person—that had no place in Nick's world. It served no purpose to the job he'd come here to do. It hindered him, actually.

He had to think of her as nothing but a subject of an investigation, a means to an end.

Period.

She was still laughing when one of her sisters showed up, pushing a baby carriage, one about the size of a small bus.

A double-seater, he realized.

There wasn't just one baby in there. There were two. Or a baby and a…what would you call it? It was still mostly bald, sucking two of its fingers on one hand, bashing the other against the bar that kept it from getting out of the hideous contraption, looking like it would break out if it could. It was dressed all in yellow, some kind of one-piece outfit that left no clue to its sex, and in between sucking on those fingers it was babbling about something. Something that made absolutely no sense.

Nick tried not to look too scary, not wanting to make it cry.

The not-quite-baby grinned up at him, like it found him every bit as amusing as a certain adult Nick knew.

The baby in the backseat was slumped over to its side in a position he felt sure would give it a bad back. Eyelids dropping, it was sucking the same fingers as the one in front, except the baby was… What was that drool coming out of it's mouth?

Oooh. It was drooling like a little waterspout.

Nick grimaced.

The whole front of its little suit was wet in a big circle around the collar.

What was up with that?

Kim greeted her sister like she hadn't seen her in weeks, when Nick knew damned well they'd had lunch together the day before. Then she turned to him to introduce him, but her sister beat her to it.

"You must Eric," she said, throwing her arms around Nick and giving him a big hug. "I'm Kim's sister, Kathie. We're so happy to have you here in Magnolia Falls. Everyone can't wait to meet you."

Nick endured as best he could, trying not to scowl about being mistaken for a pirate/terrorist, part of him wondering how in the hell Kim's sister could think she was involved with someone as old and broken-down as Nick felt. Part of him wishing it didn't seem like such a ridiculous idea. Even if he couldn't have her, just thinking that it might be possible for him to have her was a scarily attractive proposition.

"Kathie, honey. No. This isn't Eric," Kim said.

Her sister pulled away, looking puzzled. "But…I thought…"

"This is Nick Cavanaugh, my new neighbor. He's staying at the B&B, Mrs. Baker's first guest. Remember me telling you she'd opened up a few days early?"

"Oh. Sure." Her sister grinned at Nick. "Sorry. I just… Well, we're all anxious to meet Kim's new boyfriend and when I saw the two of you and Kim looking so happy, I just assumed you were him."

"No problem," Nick said, knowing she was not going to be happy for long with her pirate.

"Nice to meet you, too." She held out a hand. "I'm Kathie Reed."

He shook her hand.

"And this is Cassie, who's almost two, and her baby brother, Ned."

Cassie held out her slobbery fingers in greeting. Nick declined what he feared was her offer of a handshake, instead keeping his distance and trying to work up a smile. Cassie pouted, but at least she didn't cry. Harry would have just loved it if *Scary Nick* showed up and made a toddler cry.

"Nick's a city planner. He's here studying the park for a town that might want to build one like it."

He tried to look city-plannerish, like a guy who liked trees and flowers and the outdoors in general, fearing he was failing wildly.

Kathie Reed frowned at him, much like her sister was prone to do. "Oh. How nice for you. We just love our park."

"Kathie was married here," Kim said.

Her sister nodded. "In the gazebo right over there, overlooking the falls. It was beautiful."

"And she got engaged here, too. And so did our parents," Kim added.

"Oh," Nick said, like he needed to make a note of that. Like he was a guy who could design a spot for romantic weddings and engagements.

Scowl, scowl, scowl.

Scary Nick.

"Well," he said, forcing a carefully neutral expression across his face. "I should make my way to the falls. I have a lot of work to do today."

"Thanks for helping me with my measurements," Kim said.

"No problem. Happy to help."

"And you'll get back to me about… the number?"

"Sure," he said. "As soon as I hear anything."

He waved to her and her sister, and off he went.

"There's something odd about that man," Kathie told Kim after they'd bought sandwiches from a snack cart in the park and settled themselves on a bench.

"I know," Kim said, unwrapping her chicken salad and pinching off a bite for her niece, who had her mouth hanging open at the ready.

Cassie took her bite and smushed it against her mouth, not quite getting it open in time, but she stayed with it until most of the sandwich ended up in the right place.

Kim grinned at her, then thought of her offbeat neighbor. "He comes off all dry and cynical, but he's really funny when you start talking to him. Still, there's something about him—"

"Something odd," Kathie insisted.

"I guess. But for some reason, I like him. He stood here for close to an hour helping me take measurements of the fountain for the mosaic."

"Okay, so he's helpful and makes you laugh. Still… does he strike you as a guy who'd plan parks for a living?"

"Not at all. He seems way too serious for that."

Cassie grabbed on to the front cushioned bar of her stroller and started trying to push it back and forth, succeeding only in pushing her own body back and forth. "Ahh-uhhh-ahhh-uhhh-ahhh," she said, like a little Tarzan-girl.

Kim gave her another bite of her sandwich. "Open up first this time," she said, trying to help.

Cassie didn't.

Her mother just sighed, took the piece from her daughter's collar and into her mouth. "We're going to figure this out one day. I'm sure of it."

Cassie chewed enthusiastically with her mouth wide open.

"We'll figure that part out, too."

"I'm sure," Kim said.

"So, I have your final student list for your art class. I'm so glad you're doing this for us. It's so hard once kids get behind and know they won't be able to graduate with their class. It makes it that much easier for them to give up and quit school altogether," her sister said.

"I'm happy to do it. And excited about the project."

Kathie was a former teacher herself, and since the birth of her first child, she'd been working part-time with Big Brothers Big Sisters as the group's education coordinator. It gave her the flexibility she needed with her kids, while still keeping her involved in education. She and Kim together had sold the school district on the idea of Kim's slightly offbeat art class, funded and coordinated by Big Brothers Big Sisters.

"If this works, I have a friend who's into metalwork. We might be able to get him to do a class that makes park benches or something like that," Kim said.

"Great."

"Gaaaiiiit," Cassie said.

"Almost, sweetie," Kim said.

Then shook her head, imagining what Nick would have to say about taking a bunch of high school kids with delinquent tendencies and giving them a blowtorch to play with. He'd love that.

"So, I'm trying not to ask, because I know everyone's bugging you about it, but where is the guy we're all dying to meet?" her sister asked.

"He'll be here soon. I know he will," Kim said with all the conviction she could muster.

She was trying not to worry. Honestly, she was.

Of course he was going to show up.

He was wonderful and he was in love with her.

It wasn't some silly holiday fling.

Why would it be that? He wouldn't have told her he loved her if it had just been that. There'd be no reason to say he was in love with her so quickly if he wasn't really in love with her.

Unless he'd just been trying to get her into bed with him.

She'd tried hard not to even consider the possibility, but the longer she waited without so much as a phone call from him, the more that thought kept creeping in.

What if he'd said it only because he'd wanted to sleep with her?

Guys did that all the time, didn't they?

"Hey, what's wrong?" her sister asked.

"Nothing." She smiled brightly, thinking she was just feeling overly emotional given all that had happened to her in a little more than two weeks. Her entire life had changed. The feelings she had for Eric were so strong and it had all happened so quickly. It was all so new, so overwhelming.

Being back here with her family without him, it was easy to almost imagine that it had never happened, that it had all been a dream.

She'd come back to her ordinary life, filled with all these new feelings, missing Eric like crazy and now…

Where was he?

Had something happened to him?

If he'd gotten into a car accident or something, no one would even know to call her, would they? Or how to get in touch with her, even if he'd mentioned her name.

"I just want Eric to be here," Kim said.

"Well, of course you do. We all want him here."

And he would be, as soon as he could get here.

That's what he'd promised.

That he had to go home, clear up a few things with work, arrange for more time off and get on the next plane for Atlanta.

What had gone wrong with that?

Kim spent the next two days catching up with her family and working on arrangements for her class. The first meeting in the park was in three days. She'd have outlines drawn to scale of the existing fountain for the kids to use as they came up with their own design ideas for the project. One of their ideas, probably with some tweaking by her and the class, would be used for the project. They only had six weeks, so they had to get moving. She wanted to start construction within two weeks.

Distracted, thinking of all she had to do to finish the project on time, she unlocked her apartment door that afternoon and walked inside, and it wasn't until she got into the kitchen that she noticed something odd.

There was something on her countertop.

She went to put her fountain plans down and felt it on the back of her hand.

Turning her hand over, she saw tiny white specks.

She sniffed.

Sugar?

Tasted.

Yes, it was sugar.

Kim frowned.

She wasn't the world's greatest housekeeper, but she wouldn't leave a trail of sugar on her countertop, either. She should know. She'd just cleaned her kitchen yesterday, and she hadn't used any sugar this morning. When she'd opened the refrigerator, she'd discovered she was out of milk, and if she couldn't have some milk in her tea, she'd do without. It just didn't taste good to her without it.

And when she didn't have tea, she didn't use sugar, unless she was baking cookies or something, which she hadn't done since she got back from her trip.

She grabbed the sugar canister and looked inside.

Nothing but sugar, it looked like.

Who would have helped themselves to sugar in her apartment?

Her sister Kate had a key, just because it seemed like a good idea for someone else to have a key, in case Kim lost hers. Her landlady had a key, and there were times when Kim felt like Mrs. O'Connor was a little more nosy than she should be. She wouldn't have been upset if Mrs. O'Connor needed to borrow some sugar, but she'd like to know about it before the woman helped herself to something inside Kim's apartment.

Kim started pulling out the other canisters, three with her favorite teas, one with coffee for guests who preferred that, one with flour, again for those rare times she made something.

It looked like there were a few coffee grounds on the counter, too, behind that canister.

Okay, someone borrowing coffee and sugar at the same time without telling her seemed even weirder.

It gave her the creeps.

She turned and scanned her apartment carefully, going into the living room, the bathroom, her bedroom. Were things just a little bit out of place on her dressing table? Perfume bottles rearranged, maybe? A stack of papers not quite as straight as they'd been when she'd left them on top of her satchel on the floor beside her nightstand? Maybe the stuff in her medicine cabinet not quite the way she'd left it?

She couldn't be sure. She'd lived in the building for three years now, first in a two-bedroom apartment she'd shared with Kathie, then in this one-bedroom alone, and never felt anything less than completely safe here. There was a newly-married couple in the apartment she and Kathie used to share, Mrs. O'Connor on the first floor and a sweet little old lady named Mrs. Beasley in the other first-floor apartment. Lizzie Watson was in the other apartment on Kim's floor.

Someone was always here and Mrs. O'Connor was as good as a watchdog. Better, even, because she could talk.

She went to find Mrs. O'Connor, but when she knocked on the woman's door, she didn't answer.

Mrs. Beasley did answer her door, as usual with a welcoming smile.

"Hello, dear, how are you?"

"Fine, Mrs. Beasley. And you?"

"I could not be better, my dear. What can I do for you today?"

"I'm looking for Mrs. O'Connor. Have you seen her?"

"She just left with her daughter to visit her granddaughter, the one who's expecting a baby soon, who lives in Macon. Why? Is there a problem?"

"No. Not really." Kim didn't want to worry Mrs. Beasley.

"I was just wondering. Did you see anyone heading upstairs today who…well, someone who's not usually here?"

Mrs. Beasley gave her an odd look, but thankfully just answered the question.

"That nice young man from the phone company was here, to check on someone's phone. I met him in the hallway as I was going for my afternoon walk," Mrs. Beasley said.

"Someone's phone was out?"

"Well, I'm not sure. He said he had to check on someone's phone."

"And he was wearing a phone company uniform?"

Mrs. Beasley nodded.

"He's the only one you saw?"

"Yes, dear. Are you sure everything's all right?"

Kim nodded, trying to look like she believed it.

"Thank you, Mrs. Beasley."

She went upstairs and checked on her phone, just to make certain nothing was wrong with it. Her first thought had been that maybe Eric hadn't called her because there was something wrong with her phone. And she wouldn't have been all that surprised if Mrs. O'Connor had let someone from the phone company into her apartment and forgot to tell her. Or that maybe the Whitakers upstairs had phone trouble, and maybe while the phone guy was here checking on their phone, he'd checked on Kim's, too, just…because.

What that had to do with her sugar container or her coffee supply, she didn't know.

But it was easier to imagine than someone searching her sugar and coffee canisters, which was just weird.

Why would anyone search anything of hers?

When she picked up her phone, it was working. She called

the Whitakers to be sure, and Betsy Whitaker answered on the second ring.

"Hi, Betsy. It's Kim from downstairs. Have you been having trouble with your phone?"

"No, why? Are you?"

"No," Kim said. "Just…well, Mrs. Beasley said someone from the phone company was here today and… Oh, never mind, Betsy. Sorry I bothered you. I'm sure it's nothing."

Did they have phone lines outside anyone's apartment? Or a phone box of some sort somewhere? Maybe wiring that someone needed to check that day?

She knew next to nothing about phone boxes or wiring or anything like that.

She just knew that her phone seemed to be working fine, that Eric hadn't called and that someone seemed to have searched her sugar and coffee canisters.

What could anyone possibly expect to find in there?

Chapter Seven

Nick was playing Peeping Tom again. As best he could considering it was daytime.

Not that he was looking forward to nighttime, either.

He wasn't looking forward to anything.

Certainly not bath time.

Torture time, as he'd come to think of it.

Did she take a bath every day? Or was that a kind of treat? A relaxation thing? An indulgence?

So far, she'd taken a bath every night.

Although her climbing out of the shower couldn't be that much better.

Nick groaned just thinking about it as he watched her look around her apartment like she'd lost something. As long as it kept her out of the bathtub, he was happy.

Harry called on Nick's cell, no doubt because Nick refused to turn on his radio. Harry could be damned irritating.

"Yeah," Nick said, sitting in his spot by the window, looking down into her apartment with grim resolve.

"I've got fifty bucks that says she takes a bath again tonight," Harry said.

"Shut up, Harry!"

"Ahhh, come on. We have to have a little fun."

"What did you find out about the phone number?" Nick asked.

"It's a cell. One of those pay-as-you-go ones, just like we suspected."

"Dammit," Nick said.

Those things would be outlawed if he had anything to say about it, because there was no friggin' paperwork. No name. No address. No nothing. Anybody could buy one at any time and call anyone else, and unless you could catch the call bouncing off a satellite somewhere because you had the party on the other side of the call under surveillance, there was no way to trace the call.

"Yeah. I know. We dialed. Guy didn't answer. The message feature has one of those weird, computerized, fake voices saying you can leave a message, so there's no voiceprint. No way to know if he's even still using the phone or if he's ditched it. Hell, he could have a dozen of these phones and never use the same one twice. We gotta figure out what to tell Little Miss Gorgeous about it."

What would be best to tell her, Harry meant. What would further their investigation?

"Okay. We tell her the truth, she's probably going to think it's odd that he'd be using a phone like that," Nick said. "Or that he has lousy credit and is a lousy prospect as a boyfriend." None of which they wanted. "We tell her the line's not working and then she's got an excuse for why he hasn't called her. Although why he wouldn't call from work or home or borrow someone's phone..."

"Believe me, I wouldn't let a phone being out of order keep me from calling her," Harry said.

"Yeah. We tell her it's a landline, she's going to want an address so she can try to find him herself—"

"Or if she has another way to contact him, she'd probably use it then."

And they needed to know if she had another way to contact him.

The only problem was, Nick didn't want her having anything to do with the guy. Not personally. Professionally he had to want her to contact the guy, if it led him and his people to the jerk.

"We don't want her suspicious, but we do want her trying to contact him," Nick said, thinking out loud. "I'm going to tell her the number's not working, but that we couldn't figure out why. Then I'll just ask if she has another way to contact him. I think she'll tell me if she does."

"'Cause she likes you?" Harry asked.

"She tolerates me."

He wasn't kidding himself about it being anything more.

"Tell her tonight," Harry said. "We need to move this thing along."

Yeah, they did.

Kim thought about calling her brother, because the whole thing with the sugar and the coffee was creeping her out. But in all likelihood it was nothing. Mrs. O'Connor forgetting to tell her she'd let the phone company guy in and the phone company getting mixed up about whose line was giving them trouble or something like that.

This was Magnolia Falls, after all.

Nothing really dangerous ever happened in Magnolia Falls.

And her brother tended to be a tad overprotective anyway. She tried not to ever give him an excuse to worry even more about her and he'd worry about this. He'd probably freak out about this. He'd come over and dust for prints, probably haul in every guy who'd worked for the phone company in the last ten years for questioning. It would not be pretty.

And he'd watch her even more closely than he already did, despite the fact that she was a completely reasonable, rational twenty-four-year-old woman, more than capable of watching out for herself, her little travel difficulties notwithstanding.

So what if she'd had her wallet, her credit cards and her traveler's checks stolen in New York City once, taken in by a fake mime in Central Park? She'd just thought he was doing some kind of magic trick, that's all, and everybody liked magic tricks, didn't they? She'd still gotten home okay. And that whole thing with the car accident in Mexico because there was a goat on the road.... That had been way overblown. It hadn't hurt her or the car that much, and there was no way she was hitting a goat. She still didn't believe that was a scam. That the goat's owner forced him out into the road at least once a day in hopes of running a tourist off the road, then scamming them into letting him fix their rental car so they didn't have to report it to the insurance company or the car-rental place. He'd been a very nice man, after all, and way too nice to the goat to shove him into the road. And she hadn't nearly drowned in Vienna. She hadn't!

But her brother was a little odd about things at times and she did not want to call him unless she absolutely had to.

So the phone company guy had made himself a cup of coffee and he liked sugar and hadn't cleaned up that well after himself?

No big deal.

She wouldn't begrudge him a cup of coffee.

She wouldn't make a federal case of it, either.

And yet, as the sun went down and darkness slowly descended around her, she hated the idea of being in her apartment alone.

She started turning on lights. All of them. She locked the door, unlocked it and locked it again. Yes, the lock was working. She had a dead bolt. It was working, too.

She was heading for the stereo, to turn it on, so she didn't have to stay there in utter silence, listening for every little thing that went bump in the night, when someone knocked on her door.

"Ahhh!" She couldn't help it. It startled her.

"Kim? Are you okay?"

It was her neighbor Nick's voice, sounding as worried as she felt.

"Kim!"

"Yes. I'm here. Hang on." She got to the door, fumbled with the lock.

Why did he sound so scared?

Had the mysterious phone guy been trespassing in his room, too?

She pulled open the door and it was like some mysterious force was pushing her forward, toward him. Like for a moment, it was all she could do not to throw herself into his arms and play the helpless, frightened female, ridiculous as that notion was.

"What's wrong?" he demanded, moving closer, his hands closing around her upper arms in a firm, reassuring grip.

"Nothing," she said, her quaking voice ruining any claim she might have made at that point.

"Don't lie to me," he said with an urgency she didn't understand and didn't like hearing. "What happened?"

"Nothing. Nothing happened."

"Kim, you're trembling," he said, still hanging on to her.

Not that she objected to that. She was still fighting the urge to curl up against his big male body. She didn't think he'd object. Oh, he'd probably be surprised and demand even more answers, but at least she'd feel safe for a moment and feeling safe sounded really good to her.

"I'm being silly," she said.

"In what way?" he said, doing that enunciating-so-carefully thing that he did, the familiar shot of impatience and irritation back in his voice.

She grinned in spite of herself, because that was Nick and the familiarity was reassuring at the moment.

"In what you'd no doubt think of as a silly, female way," she said, feeling much better now that he was here.

He didn't seem amused. Or even remotely satisfied by her answer.

If anything, it irritated him even more.

His mouth stretched into a grim line, and his eyes went all smoky and dark and...interesting.

He was a very interesting man. She couldn't deny it.

She wasn't interested, she told herself. She was in love, after all.

But it didn't render a woman blind to every other man in the universe.

She could say with complete objectivity that he was a very interesting, even attractive, man.

He looked like a man who couldn't quite figure out what to do with her. His hands were still locked on her arms in a grip that was firm, yet reassuring and somehow even gentle.

There was heat radiating from his body, which didn't seem hampered or injured in any way at the moment. And the idea of curling up against him while she caught her breath—tried to catch her breath—and stopped shaking was almost more than she could deny.

"You can tell me," he said, his voice going soft and deep, impossibly compelling.

She inched closer just a bit, took a breath and tried to let it out with deliberate, calming slowness.

"I know something scared you. I have trouble thinking it was simply because I knocked on your door. Surely lots of people come and see you. I bet they all knock on your door, that it's not something that normally frightens you."

Kim hovered there, blessedly close to him, confused, tempted, irritated with herself and with Eric for not being here when he should be—still feeling a bit scared and silly and just not knowing what to do.

"Someone scared you?" Nick asked.

"No," she whispered.

"Something?"

She nodded.

"Tell me," he said. "Tell me what happened."

An invitation that sounded impossibly appealing. Nearly as appealing as resting for a moment in his arms.

He drew her to him, then, little by little, inch by inch, giving her all the time in the world to object or to pull away. Pulled her to him so slowly that she wondered if he had to fight himself to let her be that close to him.

It felt oddly sexual and oddly not.

Sexually charged, actually, and yet like he was erecting some kind of wall between them, touching her and yet not letting himself really touch her.

She got to where her forehead brushed against his chin and then her chin rubbed against the top of his shoulder as she turned her head away from him and laid her head against the surprisingly hard muscles of his chest. Ever so slowly, she let her body rest against the strength of his, reassured and a little bit scared.

It felt good.

Really good.

Better than it should have, she decided, to a woman newly fallen in love with the man of her dreams.

Who was not here, hadn't been here, showed no signs of coming here.

And yet, she loved him, didn't she?

Eric, her savior from the ship?

Did a woman in love get to feel this good in the arms of another man? Even if it had started out in a completely innocent way? Even if she was scared?

Kim wasn't sure.

She'd never been in love before.

"What happened?" Nick demanded, the voice nothing at all like the way he held her in his arms.

His arms were pure strength, reassurance, acceptance, as if there to serve her every whim, standing ready to fulfill any need she might have. His voice was harsh, demanding, impatient to the core. The incongruity of it registered on some level, but she had too many other things to figure out to puzzle over it for long.

"It's silly," she said, her arms at his waist, hands curling around fistfuls of his shirt. If he tried to move away, she feared she'd hang on for dear life to keep those arms of his around her.

She shuddered once, then again, couldn't help it, and sank against him.

His whole body seemed to go on alert, tension in every pore. It was like she could feel him searching the apartment behind her as best he could, ready to spring into action.

What in the world?

"Tell me," he said. "Tell me now, so I can take care of it."

He could?

He would?

What did he think happened? And how could he take care of it?

Although having someone do just that sounded really good to her.

"I think someone's been in my apartment," she said.

"Been here? Or is still here?"

"Been here and gone."

"You checked?" he demanded.

"I checked."

He pushed her to the side, grabbed at his shoulder, his hand fumbling there, then hesitating. What was it with him and that shoulder?

"Stay behind me," he said. "I want to check for myself, just to be sure."

"You think he's still in here?" she yelled.

"I want to be sure, Kim. Humor me."

He didn't say it like a man wanting someone to humor him. He said it like a man used to giving orders and having them obeyed.

What kind of orders did a guy who planned parks for a living normally give?

Kim followed him anyway, because she didn't want to be anywhere alone and she figured the safest place for her was right next to him. He searched every nook and cranny of her apartment, much in the same way she could picture her brother doing if she'd called him with her crazy story about the phone guy and stray coffee grounds.

When he was finally satisfied they were alone, he closed her apartment door and locked it, then took her by the hand and led her to the sofa, sat her down on it, then sat on the edge of the coffee table, facing her and said, "Tell me everything. Now."

"You'll think I'm being silly," she said, now that she knew no one was here except him and her, and she'd stopped shaking.

"Do I look like a man who finds many things even remotely silly?"

"No."

"Then give it your best shot. Try to amuse me," he said.

Kim's mouth twitched, aching to smile, because it was so very Nick-like, even if his recent behavior was not. For a moment, it was like he was someone else completely, someone she couldn't begin to know. Like Clark Kent in the old movies turning into Superman in a whirl, a cape and the lack of his dorky glasses making all the difference in the world.

She'd always found the notion ludicrous until now.

"Kim—"

"Okay. Okay. I'll tell you. I came home and found sugar and coffee grounds on my kitchen countertop."

He gave her a look that said, "And?"

"And I didn't make that mess. I don't even drink coffee. I drink tea. I keep coffee for people who come over and have to have coffee, but I haven't had anyone here drinking coffee since before my trip and I just cleaned the kitchen last night. I didn't spill the sugar or coffee and I don't know who did. Except maybe for the phone guy—"

"Phone guy?"

"Except, there's nothing wrong with my phone that I know of. So why was the phone guy here?"

"A phone repairman was here? In your apartment?"

"I think so," she said. "Otherwise, who would have made a mess of the coffee?"

Coffee grounds?

Phone repairmen where there was nothing wrong with phones?

Nick stared at the woman who'd just scared him half out of his mind, trying to think through the fear, to make sense of what she was saying, but it just wasn't happening.

Still, she was right in front of him, safe and sound. Just scared, that was all. She wasn't shaking anymore. She wasn't in his arms, thank goodness. And she wasn't making a whole lot of sense, but she was okay.

"Start over," he said. "Slowly, so that maybe I can understand. You came home, and…?"

"Found sugar and coffee grounds on the kitchen countertop. Like someone had searched the sugar and the coffee canisters and made a mess while they did it. Why would anyone be trying to find anything in my sugar or coffee supply?"

"I have no idea," he said. "But keep going. You found the mess…"

"And I knew I hadn't made it, which means someone else had to. Which means, someone must have been in here."

"Okay." He was starting to get it. Who'd been here? Maybe the love of her life? The pirate?

"So I looked around the apartment—"

He grimaced, just thinking about that. The woman believed someone had been in her apartment and what did she do? She went looking for him! Sure. That's what any reasonable person would do, right? Go see if they could find the guy who'd broken in?

"Go on," he said, snarling, *Scary Nick* back in full force.

"What?" she demanded.

"He could have still been here, Kim," Nick roared.

She flinched, looked hurt, looked like she might cry.

"And don't you dare cry," he said.

Her lower lip started to tremble. Tears filled her eyes as she glared at him. "I'm already scared enough without you yelling at me."

Which meant that—dammit—he was probably going to touch her again, try to reassure her again and then try very, very, very hard not to do anything else when he had her that close to him. Which he figured was next to impossible, but he was going to give it a shot, because she was scared and Scary Nick had yelled at her and made her cry.

"Oh, hell. I'm sorry," he said. "You scared me, too."

She bent her head down, like she didn't want him to see her tears and he leaned forward until he found himself with her head on his shoulder, his arms cradling her in a loose embrace which he found thoroughly unsatisfying.

He just sat there, his head bent down to hers, her shoulders shaking while she cried and shook and buried her nose in the crook of his neck. She smelled sweet and her skin was so soft—from the bath he supposed and that stuff she'd smoothed all over herself afterward. He fought the urge to bury his face in her hair and kiss her cheek, her closed eyes, her nose. Her mouth. Anything. Any part of her.

"It's all right now," he said, even though it wasn't. Even though she was in danger even while he was here. He was supposed to be the one protecting her and someone had gotten in here and done who knew what in her apartment.

He ran his hands up and down her back in a move he hoped was soothing and not too personal, not too tempting to himself, tried very hard not to think of what it felt like to have his hands on her, on all that he'd seen of that tempting body of hers while he'd been spying on her on the ship and here in her own apartment. Tried not to think of all the things he wanted and could not have.

Sometimes it seemed like his whole life had been about nothing but things he'd wanted and could not have.

There'd been women who couldn't handle his job and the life he led, women he might have been able to build a life with, a brother he hardly ever saw, nieces and nephews who wouldn't have known him from a stranger on the street, a mother working on her fifth marriage and a father who'd disappeared when Nick was six.

He hadn't planned on having this sort of life. It had just happened, and it had worked fine for a long time.

Still, there were things he wished were different, things that could have been simple, could have been real.

She was quickly making her way to the very top of the list of things that could have been real.

Scary Nick didn't get women like her.

Still, she was right here with him now, easing closer he feared and in no hurry to stop crying or move away.

He debated with himself for all of half a second longer, then in one move, shifted around to sit on the sofa and pull her more fully into his arms.

Honestly, that's all he meant to do.

But somehow in the shift from one spot to another, she ended up sitting in his lap, her arms wrapped around him like she might never let him go. He saw big, dark eyelashes spiked together with tears, a trail of moisture running down her soft cheeks, her sexy-as-hell lower lip puffed out in a little pout that sent a purely sexual ache shooting throughout his entire body in a flash.

That silly phrase, *You're beautiful when you cry,* ran through his head, then, *You're beautiful all the time.*

And then he gave in and kissed her.

Oh, God, he was kissing her.

His mouth found hers, surprised her, he realized. Maybe even startled her. She jumped a little, sighed, made a little whimpering sound in the back of her throat that he decided was the sexiest thing he'd ever heard. Her lips parted ever so slightly, pressed against his. They were wet with her tears and he set himself to the task of finding all those tears and kissing them away. From her mouth, her cheeks, her eyes, her chin.

And then he just devoured her.

One minute she was sitting on his lap, scared, and the next he was easing her back against the sofa and following her down, bodies tangled together, until they were lying on the sofa, his mouth locked on hers.

It was like diving into a banquet. He didn't know where to start.

Her soft, soft lips, her hair, the smell of her skin, all those sweet curves laid out beneath him.

She opened herself to him and he let himself sink into her, stroking her, tasting her, teasing her. His hand caught in her hair, holding her to him, the other slid down her side and palmed her hips, fitting her body to his.

He would have begged happily at that point.

Right here. Just stay right here. Just for a minute. Please.

He thought she was okay with that, thought her hands were clutching at his back, urging him closer. He hoped that wasn't pure wishful thinking on his part. And she was definitely kissing him back. Yes, she was. Her mouth opened to his as he thrust into her in the only way he could allow himself at the moment.

But he was thinking of other ways he might be doing this, was thinking of what it would take to get her clothes off and his and truly be inside of her in no time flat and how that would feel and how soon they might do it again, her climbing out of the tub and walking toward him dripping wet and him giving up, giving in, gone.

He dragged himself off of her, feeling like a sixteen-year-old looking at a girlie magazine.

He had no control whatsoever.

Dammit, he muttered.

Not that he could get away. She was still sprawled out across his lap, their bodies all twisted together. He could sit up, breathing hard, still turned on as hell, but he couldn't get away.

She lay there with her head against the big, cushy arm of the sofa, her arms wrapped around herself, like she wanted to protect herself from him. She shot him an accusing look he rightly deserved. A look that said, *What in the world was that!* That said, *One minute I was terrified and just wanted you to help me and the next you were on top of me, you rat!*

He noted that he wasn't the only one struggling to breathe normally. That her cheeks were flushed and her eyes were dry, at least.

And her mouth… *Oh, that mouth.*

Yum.

Just yum.

It was an absolutely juvenile word, Nick knew, but the only one he could come up with that fit.

It was all he could do not to dive back on top of her right

that minute and beg her to let him do anything…just anything she'd permit. Teenage boys begged, too, he remembered. Begged very well.

And in her life, she wasn't that far removed from having teenage boys begging for all sorts of things from her, while he…he had a body that was threatening to fall apart. He was limping, for God's sake, and grumpy, sometimes scary and old, fast becoming a bad cliché, the old man lusting after the pretty little girl.

Just shoot me now, he thought.

Please.

She was looking at him finally, waiting for some explanation, no doubt. Looking hurt and sad and surprised all at the same time.

Surprised in a good way? Nick wondered before he could help himself. *Surprised like… she'd liked it?*

Not that it mattered in the least.

Not that he'd ever be doing this again.

Not like he didn't have one hell of an apology he had to offer and fast, and then do some quick talking to try to explain and have her keep trusting him and talking to him.

How was he going to manage that?

Nick shook his head back and forth, at a complete loss. "I'm sorry," he said.

She frowned. "Okay."

"Okay?" He wanted to believe that. "You mean, it's okay—"

"No. It's not okay. I just meant…okay, you're sorry. What else?"

"I don't know. I just…lost it for a minute." That was certainly true. "I didn't mean to do it. I can't believe I did."

"Okay," she said again.

"Okay? Like…not at all okay? Like…what do you have to say from there, asshole?"

She nodded. "That works."

He was afraid of that. "I don't know what else, okay? I just don't know. You were scared and I was here and I just didn't want you to be scared anymore and I was sorry I made it worse by yelling at you and then…I don't know. You're….well, you know what you are and I'm just a man. You know what men are like, too, right?"

Her mouth fell open, in what he feared was disbelief and a definite dissatisfaction with his answer.

What had he even said? He honestly wasn't sure at the moment.

If he could just walk through that door right now and start all over again, he was sure he could handle this whole thing better. The only problem was, then he wouldn't have gotten to kiss her and snuggle on the couch with her and he didn't think he'd give that up for anything in this world. Not even if it meant not having to sit here, completely baffled, trying to explain the whole thing to her.

"I'm sorry," he said again.

And he was.

Because she was not happy and he had honestly just wanted to help her and he'd made things worse. Or different. Or uncomfortable. Or odd.

"That's it? That's your explanation? You're a man and I know what men are like?"

He nodded. "Best one I've got, I'm afraid."

"And I'm…what? What is it that I'm supposed to know about myself?"

"That you're gorgeous," he said in all honesty. "That you make grown men weep by walking down the street. By just existing. By breathing. By walking into a room. You are drop-dead one-hundred-percent gorgeous and men must have been making fools of themselves over you since the day you were born, so I have a hard time believing you could be that surprised by this. By one more man behaving like…a man."

He glanced over at her.

She still looked pissed.

"Neanderthal man," he tried. "Caveman. Jerk-of-a-man. Grabbing you and rolling around on the sofa with you. Taking advantage of you—"

"Like a man? Because that's what men are like? That's it? Your entire explanation?"

"We try to do better most of the time. Honestly, we do, but yeah…like a man." He frowned, sighed, wished he could just disappear. "I mean…I know you think I'm old enough to be half-dead, but trust me, I'm not that old. Not enough to be immune to a woman like you."

Chapter Eight

Kim felt a little like she had when the pirates attacked.

Because who got attacked by pirates?

No one did.

They were pirates, for heaven's sake.

But there she'd been, getting attacked by pirates and not quite believing it was happening.

For the second time in as many weeks, she found herself trying to clear her head and not quite sure how to connect one thing that had happened with the next, not quite able to figure out how she'd gotten from point *A* to point *B*.

Point *B* being Nick kissing her silly.

"I'm sorry," he said again. "Really. I am."

"Okay," she said, for lack of anything better to say, anything even remotely coherent.

She was reminded instantly of an old boyfriend she'd caught kissing her best friend when Kim was sixteen, after he'd pledged his supposedly undying love for her. She hadn't bought the undying-love bit, but she had liked him more than anyone she'd ever dated and she'd thought he was a good guy. So she'd been surprised and hurt and angry to find him rolling around on the rec-room floor with Shelly Stevens. And when he came to try to apologize, all he'd managed to come up with was, *I don't know how that happened.*

Sure, Kim had thought. *Right. You have no idea how you ended up kissing her that way. Sure you don't.*

But if Eric had walked in right that minute or one of her sisters or her brother, she'd have said practically the same thing.

I have no idea how that happened. Why it happened. What it meant. What I'm going to do about it.

How it possibly could have felt so very good.

Kim made a face.

"Are you going to cry again?" Nick said with his trademark gruffness that she somehow found both appealing and amusing.

"I don't think so. Why?"

"Because…" He shrugged helplessly. "Because I don't want you to. Because I hope you're not. And because it's hard to watch you cry and for me not to do something about it. Which we've already established that you probably wouldn't like. So I'm hoping you won't do that again, so that I won't do the other thing again. So I won't make things even worse. Sorry."

"Okay," she said.

Don't cry and he wouldn't kiss her again?

That seemed straightforward enough. Reasonable enough. Manageable enough.

She would not cry.

And she'd try to forget how it had felt to be kissed by her very unusual neighbor, Nick Cavanaugh.

"Can we get back to your mysterious sugar thief?"

"He didn't steal any sugar," she said.

"You know what I mean."

"Yes," she said, wondering how what he'd just said could come off so completely like a gruff kind of kindness, that she could feel like she understood it so completely and was so sure that's what it was. Kindness. Concern. Outright worry.

She liked the idea of him worrying about her.

Of him caring.

Nick gave a sigh of complete exasperation and Kim tried not to grin at him and let him know that she somehow found that an attractive trait as well.

"So there was a guy from the phone company in your apartment?" he asked.

"I think so."

"Why do you think so?"

"Because someone was here, obviously, and when I went to find my landlady, Mrs. O'Connor, she wasn't here, but the lady who lives in the apartment next to my landlady, Mrs. Beasley, was. She said she'd seen a man from the phone company go upstairs, that he said he had to check on someone's phone. And there aren't that many of us upstairs. Mrs. O'Connor's apartment has an upstairs and a downstairs, so she has part of this floor, and Lizzie Watson and I have one-bedrooms here. A married couple, the Whitakers live on the third floor."

"And you asked them about it?"

Kim nodded. "Betsy said there's nothing wrong with their phone."

"Okay," Nick said.

"And it could be nothing. I mean, there could be something wrong with someone else's phone. There could have been something wrong with mine that I didn't know about. The phone guy could have fixed it before I even knew it wasn't working. But..."

"What?" Nick asked.

"I don't know. You'll think it's silly—"

He shook his head. "Remember? I don't do silly."

And then she knew it was okay to tell him. That he wouldn't think she was silly. That he'd understand.

"It felt so creepy. I think...no, I'm pretty sure someone's been here...been through my things." She shuddered, just thinking about it.

Nick saw it, too. He tensed, like a man bracing himself against all enemies, seen and unseen.

Or a man who knew she was upset and didn't want to do anything about it?

Did he still want to do something about her being upset?

Because he was worried about her?

Because he cared?

She liked that he cared and the fact that he was here. Liked it very much, even though she probably shouldn't.

"Then, we'll proceed as if someone's been in here. Which means we need to talk to someone at the phone company."

Kim nodded. She wanted him to do something about this, to help her figure it out and to not leave her alone just yet. To care. Even if he had kissed her when he shouldn't have. When no one should. Except Eric. Who wasn't here and hadn't called and was really starting to worry her and make her mad.

"I could call my brother," she told Nick. "But he gets a little weird where I'm concerned. He thinks I'm still twelve years old and need a mother and a father to take care of me, and since we don't have either one anymore, he thinks he has to do everything. He'd make a federal case out of this."

"Okay. No brother. Know anybody at the phone company?"

Kim shook her head.

"Want me to call my friend?" Nick offered.

"You think he could help? I mean…he's not here in town, right?"

Nick shrugged and started babbling. "Phone company cooperation thing. He can call any phone company practically anywhere and find out what he needs. There's like a…phone company interagency cooperation code. They take care of each other."

"Okay," Kim said. "Thanks."

Phone Company Interagency Cooperation Code?

Lame, he'd told himself. *Very, very lame.*

And yet she'd bought it without question.

Nick was surprised, but grateful.

He feared he was making very little sense at the moment, feared his brain was still short-circuited from touching her the way he had and wanting to do it again.

He got her out of the room on the pretense of asking her to do a more thorough search of her bedroom and bathroom, to make sure nothing had been taken and to look for any other signs that someone had truly searched her apartment.

He feared someone definitely had and that it had everything to do with her pirate/lover boy who hadn't disappeared at all, just hadn't let her know he or someone who was working with him was in town, except for the sloppy search of her apartment. Even worse was the idea that the person who did it might have been interrupted by her in the midst of it.

So why was he here? What would he want from her apartment?

It put a whole new spin on why she needed to be watched.

If she had something he wanted or needed, if he'd maybe slipped something into her luggage that he'd feared not being able to get into the country himself, then there was no telling what kind of danger she might be in, especially if the guy couldn't find what he was looking for.

Maybe they had taken something from the ship, something someone hadn't reported stolen yet—or the kind of thing one didn't report stolen—and Nick just hadn't heard about it yet. Maybe he had no idea what he was dealing with and needed to figure it out quick.

He pulled out his phone and called Harry, who answered on the first ring.

"Did you have someone search her apartment today without telling me?" Nick growled.

"No," Harry said.

"And we had somebody watching the apartment all day?"

"Of course we did."

Which meant there'd be a detailed record, including photographs, of everyone who came and went from the building. *Good.* If lover boy had been there, they'd have a very recent photo of him.

"See anybody in a phone company repairman uniform?" Nick asked.

"Give me a second. I'll check."

"And check with the phone company here in town, just in case they had someone here for legitimate reasons," Nick ordered.

"Sure. I'll do it. You okay, Nick? You sound...I don't know. All shook up."

Which made Nick think of the old Elvis song, "All Shook Up." Which he was sure she'd never heard of, because she hadn't been alive long enough. Would she even know who Elvis was, let alone how well that particular song fit him right now?

He scowled, grateful that she wasn't here to see it.

"Yeah, Harry," he admitted. "I'm a mess. Call me back when you've looked over everyone who was here today. And check with the phone company here in town. Someone claiming to be from the phone company was here. Find out if it was legitimate."

"No one from the phone company in town was here today," Nick told her an hour later, when Harry called back.

She looked a little panicked at that.

Nick managed not to grab her and hang on to her, but just barely.

"What do we do now?" she whispered, truly scared and looking so vulnerable.

How could anyone want to hurt her?

Nick hated that she was scared, wanted to tear someone limb-from-limb for making her feel this way.

Hated even more that he needed for her to stay right here and wait for Eric Weyzinski to call her or come see her or come back to get whatever it was that he'd been looking for earlier.

No way Nick was going to do that.

"Let's get out of here," he said, taking her by the arm and steering her toward the door. "You can think about it while we go get some food or something. How about that?"

She looked grateful.

And supremely kissable.

Nick could feel his brain start to short-circuit, could feel little bursts of static all throughout his head, normal thought processes disappearing with each little fizzle of stray energy.

How was he supposed to think rationally around her?

How did any man?

* * *

Kim went with him because she wanted to get out of her apartment and she didn't want to be alone. So she'd be with him.

They drove his miniscule red sports car the eight blocks to the Corner Diner, and she was happy they hadn't walked, happy not to be out on the street where mysterious sugar-searching, non-phone-company guys could be.

What in the world did they want with her?

She had an odd feeling that Nick knew more than he was telling her—maybe exactly what the non-phone-company guy wanted from her—but why would he know? What did he have to do with anything? He was a parks planner who happened to be staying at the B&B next door.

Wasn't he?

Kim wasn't sure anymore. She wasn't sure about anything.

But she let him lead her into the diner, felt eye after eye drawn to them as the owner, Darlene, led them to a table smack-dab in the center of the restaurant, where everyone could see them. Which made Kim feel a bit safer, actually. Who'd try to get to her in the Corner Diner with everyone watching?

Who'd want to get to her anyway?

Darlene left them with menus and a highly speculative glance. "Are you sure this isn't your young man?" she said.

Kim blinked up at her. "Of course I'm sure. This is Nick."

"Sure he is. It's just that ever since you've been back, the only person anyone's seen you with is him," Darlene said.

"He's just a friend. He's staying at Mrs. Baker's B&B," Kim said, trying to make herself believe it as she said it.

Nick shot Darlene what Kim was sure was a practiced I'm-just-the-guy-next-door look.

Practiced being the operative word.

He'd used that look on her before, hadn't he?

And he hadn't looked anything like a mild-mannered parks planner when he'd burst into her apartment and then searched every inch of it. He'd looked completely different. Intent in a way that frightened her. Serious as could be. Maybe even a little bit scared.

What would scare him about someone searching her sugar canister?

"I don't understand any of this," she whispered to him, once Darlene was gone.

Then he gave her his mild-mannered I-know-nothing look. "Understand what?"

"Any. Of. This," she said, hitting and pausing on each word. "Don't pretend you don't know what I'm talking about. What's going on?"

"I don't know—"

"But you know something. I know you do. And you're going to tell me right now or…or—"

"Or what?" he said, all mild-manneredness gone.

"Or I'll scream. Right here in the diner and then everyone will want to know what's going on." Her voice rose on the end and she could feel all eyes in the place shift to them once again, if people had ever stopped watching.

All her fault, too.

Going on a simple vacation and getting attacked by pirates!

Falling in love and not being shy about telling anyone and everyone about it and then not being able to produce said love-of-her-life once she returned.

"Tell me," she demanded. "Tell me now. Or else."

"Okay. Okay. Just…keep your voice down."

"Why? Everyone's already staring. They'll be staring whether or not I whisper to you. They all just want to know what's going on. Where Eric is. Whether I'm crazy to believe

I could fall in love with someone that quickly, which...maybe I was. Maybe I was just stupid. I don't know, because I can't find him now. I haven't heard a word from him and all of a sudden you seem to be everywhere I am and there's just something...odd about you. Who are you? What's going on?"

"I'm not sure," he began.

"Don't tell me that! Don't you dare tell me that—!"

"But I found out something about the phone number you gave me," he rushed on.

"You did?"

He nodded.

"That's why you showed up at my door? To tell me about Eric's phone number?"

He nodded again.

"Okay," she said, feeling moderately foolish at least and a little afraid to know what he'd found out.

"Did he tell you it was his home phone number, Kim?"

"I don't know..." She frowned, trying to remember exactly what he'd said.

"Well, it's not his home phone," Nick said.

"Okay." She thought about it for a minute. "Maybe he didn't actually say it was his home number. I mean...I thought it was, but....I don't remember, okay? I don't. He just gave me his number. Maybe I assumed it was his home number. I... Why wouldn't he give me his home number? He's supposed to be in love with me."

She sounded really pathetic there at the end, but what could she do? She'd opened her mouth and out it had come.

If he loved her, surely he'd give her his stupid home phone number.

"It's a cell," Nick said.

Kim made a face. "So? Tons of people have cells instead of landlines these days. No big deal."

"Maybe not," Nick said. "But it's not a regular cell. There's no paperwork associated with it. No records. It's one of those pay-as-you-go phones you can buy anywhere. Nobody knows your name, your address, anything. You buy a card with call time on it and use that, so the calls are virtually untraceable."

"So? Who'd want to trace his calls?"

"It's not that. It's just… They're expensive to use, especially as someone's primary phone. Most people use them if they want a phone for emergencies only or if they have credit problems and it's hard for them to get a regular cell. It's an odd choice."

"Well…still…I don't see that it really means anything. So he uses a pay-as-you-go phone? Maybe he's just disciplined. Maybe he thinks cell phones are a ridiculous luxury or an abomination against nature and free time or something. Some people are militant about them. He could object on perfectly reasonable moral grounds. So what?"

"I don't know," Nick said. "But my friend couldn't find any other phone registered to him anywhere in California."

"So what? Maybe he doesn't like talking on the phone." Maybe that's why he hadn't called her, the supposed love-of-her-life.

It sounded lame, even to her, but there it was.

"What's going on?" she asked, feeling pitiful and scared and sad.

All she'd done was fall in love. With a brave man who'd saved her from the pirates. That was all.

Everybody fell in love.

Why couldn't she do it without it turning into a disaster?

That's what it felt like. Like it was turning into a disaster.

"I don't know what's going on, but I don't like it that someone was in your apartment," Nick said.

"You're sure someone was?"

He nodded.

"How can you be sure?" she asked. Because it all seemed kind of silly now. Spilled sugar? What was a little spilled sugar?

"Because I believe you," Nick said. "I believe you're scared. I believe you know someone was in your apartment when they shouldn't have been there and there has to be a reason for that. I want to find out what it is."

"You do?"

"Yes," he said.

"You're a parks planner," she said. "What do you care who's in my apartment?"

"I just do," he said.

"Why?"

"Well…you're a nice woman and you're right next door to me. I mean…neighborliness alone…the Neighborly Code—"

"Neighborly Code?"

"Isn't there one? I could swear someone here told me about the Neighborly Code," he claimed. "You help take care of your neighbor. Especially in a small town. Isn't there some Small Town Neighborly Code? And you are right next door. If I don't help figure out what's going on, the next thing I know, someone might be searching my sugar canister—"

"You don't have a sugar canister. You're renting a room next door to me—"

"Well, Mrs. Baker's sugar canister. I know she has one. I've seen it. And she seems like a nice woman—"

"She drives you crazy. She told me so—"

"Still, she's my neighbor. My landlady. And I have an obligation—"

"Under the Landlady Code?" Kim suggested.

"Hey, don't mock the Code."

He said it with all seriousness, all sincerity, and all of a sudden Kim didn't know whether to laugh or cry.

It all struck her as ridiculous and scary and sad and just…not right.

Something was definitely not right.

"No, no, no," Nick said. "Don't do that. Especially not here. Don't cry here."

"Why not?" she said, her bottom lip quivering, tears threatening.

"Because it's bad. Everyone will stare—"

"They're already staring," she said, choking back a sob.

"Well don't give them any more reasons to stare."

"I can't help it. Something's wrong. I know it. And you know it, too, but you won't tell me. This is my life, Nick. If anybody has a right to know, surely it's me. Tell me what's going on. Where's Eric?"

"I don't know."

"But you know something. Something about him and the phone and whoever was in my apartment today—"

"I have no idea who was in your apartment today—"

"But the rest of it. You know something about the rest of it," she accused. And she was right. She could tell. "Oh, God. What's going on?"

At which point, Nick took her by the arm and half led, half dragged her out of the restaurant.

"What are you doing?" she yelled when they got onto the sidewalk and came to a dead stop, dead center on the sidewalk in front of the restaurant. People were watching through the window. She could tell.

"I'm taking you somewhere where we can talk?"

"No!"

"Do you really want to do this on a public sidewalk? Or in the diner?" he asked.

Steely-eyed Nick was back. The Nick she'd caught a glimpse of in her apartment earlier.

It scared her a little.

Maybe a lot.

Her heart started pounding. She couldn't quite breathe, didn't understand, was afraid to even know.

"You're scaring me," she whispered.

"Good. You should be scared," he said, then backed up and took a breath, reconsidering. "I mean… I don't want you to be scared. Not of me. You don't have anything to be afraid of with me. But Eric…maybe with him."

"What about him?"

"Kim, just come to the B&B with me, okay? You know Mrs. Baker. You'll feel safe there, right?"

Kim nodded.

"Okay, let's go there and I'll tell you everything I can," he said, then turned and started walking the half block to his car.

She followed him, thinking about it. What if Mrs. Baker wasn't there? What if he'd…done something to her? What if he was going to do something to Kim? Would he? Nick? Really?

"My brother's a cop," she said as threateningly as possible.

He turned around and smiled. "I know."

"And my father was a cop. He was killed in a convenience-store robbery when I was just a baby and if you know anything at all about cops, you know that they look out for their own. They especially look out for the families of other cops who've been killed doing their job."

"I know," Nick said.

"You know that's how it works? Or you know my father was a cop?"

"Both," he said, unlocking the car and holding open the door for her.

"How?"

"Are you kidding? You know how people here talk. Everybody in this town knows you and that your father was a cop who was killed in a robbery. Ten people probably told me that story alone," he said. "Can we get in the car now and go to the B&B? And talk about this there?"

"I don't know," she said.

He pulled out his cell phone and held it out to her. "Or you can call your brother right now, if that's what you want. Tell him your story. Let him make a federal case out of it, if that's what you want."

She stared at the phone for a long time, thinking it through. Her brother would make a federal case out of it. Her whole family would. If she was wrong and this was nothing, she'd be hearing about it for months at the very least and she'd fought hard for years to have her family see her as an adult, a strong, smart, capable woman and not the baby of the family.

So calling her brother would not be her preference.

Nick waited, surely more patient than a man out to do her harm would be.

The whole situation was odd, but she really couldn't imagine being in any kind of danger from Nick.

"All right," she said, getting in the car. "I'll come with you."

Chapter Nine

She didn't want to go inside with him, so they ended up sitting on the patio in the fading light, some kind of night creatures making a racket all around them. If Nick wasn't mistaken, Mrs. Baker was hovering in the kitchen, probably with a window open, listening to their conversation or waiting for Nick to drop dead. One or the other.

He wasn't sure which was more annoying, her eavesdropping or her obsession with his supposedly poor health.

Or saying too much to Kim like a damned amateur and being stuck with having to come up with something to tell her that wasn't quite the truth, but would keep her from asking too many questions for the time being. And hopefully help keep her safe.

"Well," she said, annoyed with him from the start, since he'd hauled her out of the restaurant that way.

Not one of his finer moves.

He still wasn't quite sure how it happened, except…she did something to him. Something really good and really bad, all at the same time. Something that made him forget what he was here to do—what he had to do—and made him want to do things like haul her into his lap and kiss her until they were both naked on her sofa.

Nick scratched his head, wondering where it had all gone so wrong. He was far from being an amateur. He didn't make mistakes like this.

"I'm sorry. I'm probably overreacting," he began, pausing to see if she was buying that or not.

Didn't seem to be.

Okay.

"I get a little paranoid sometimes. I try to not go there, but, well, it's a flaw of mine," he tried.

"You're telling me you have a personality flaw that tends toward paranoia and that's all that's going on here?"

Okay, it was weak, he knew, but he had trouble thinking around her and he was worried about her. If that man had gotten to her and hurt her, while Nick was here supposedly watching her and keeping her safe, he'd have never forgiven himself. It had shaken him up, knowing someone had gotten into her apartment despite how closely Nick's team was watching her.

He was going to be chewing people out left and right when he got done with her.

"I'm just saying…I might have overreacted," he said.

"About believing me that someone was in my apartment?"

"No. Not about that. But our witness, who said the guy she saw was someone from the phone company, is what? Seventy years old?"

"Sixty-three."

"Okay. Sixty-three. How's her eyesight?"

"I don't know," Kim said.

"How's her hold on reality?"

"Just fine."

"Okay, but still... She said she thought it was a guy from the phone company. What if it was some other guy in a uniform and she only got a glance at him and thought it as a guy from the phone company?" Nick tried.

"No. She said she talked to him. He said he was there to fix someone's phone."

"Well, how's her hearing?" Nick said, backed into a corner. "I mean, she's sixty-three...."

Kim looked like she was about to bash him over the head with something. "Would you just tell me what's going on?"

"I don't know," he claimed. And really, he didn't. He had suspicions. A lot of suspicions. And they might be right or they might be wrong. He didn't know yet. "But I want to check some things out, if it's okay with you."

She made a face at him. "What kind of things?"

"Like trying to find out who this guy was, who was at your apartment."

"And how would we do that?"

Fingerprints for one. Harry should have been in there and dusted the place while Nick and Kim were at the restaurant. Of course, he couldn't tell her that. And he hoped Harry was a lot more careful with the sugar than Kim's intruder had been.

"We could talk to your neighbors again. You and I together," Nick began. "If you're with me and they know we're trying to find out something for you, I think they'd be more likely to talk."

Because so far, his guys were having a hard time getting any information that they could trust to be truthful. The town was full of suspicious busybodies who loved to gossip with each other, but none of whom could get their stories straight. It was really annoying. And forget asking questions outright if you were a stranger and were asking about someone in town. They all clammed right up.

"Okay, I guess we could ask some questions together," Kim said.

"And we could talk to someone at the electric company, the gas company, the water company. All those companies, just to make sure this wasn't someone who had a legitimate reason to be there. I mean your neighbor could have bad hearing, and someone from the gas company could have been there and just not notified you. Things like that happen."

Sure they did.

"Okay," Kim said, still looking skeptical.

"And I was thinking it wouldn't be a bad idea if you stayed here tonight. Mrs. Baker's a friend, right, and she has a bunch of empty rooms. I'm probably being overcautious, but there's no reason for you to be in that apartment all by yourself until we know for sure what's going on."

Which would put her right down the hall from him.

Which wouldn't make for the most comfortable night in the world for him, but he wasn't leaving her alone over there, either.

"What do you think?" he asked.

"Well...I guess...I could stay here."

"Good—"

"I mean, I'm probably being silly, but—"

"Cautious. You're being cautious. Cautious is good in situations like this. I feel much better. I would have worried with you over there all alone," he admitted.

"You would have?"

Nick nodded, thinking, *Please don't look at me like that. Like you want me to worry about you. Like you like the idea. Like you want me to care.*

"Okay," she said. "I'll talk to Mrs. Baker about staying here."

"Good," Nick said.

It was good.

He'd lock himself in his room if he had to.

He would be okay.

At least, he thought he'd be okay.

Until she got this look on her face, this…

What was she going to do?

She looked a little uneasy, a little scared, scared in a completely different way than she had been when they'd been talking about the mysterious sugar thief.

"What?" he asked.

"Nothing. I just…" She took a step closer, looking unsure of herself. "You kissed me!"

It came out like an accusation.

"Yes," he said. No arguing with that. He'd kissed her, God help him.

"Why?"

"I told you, I don't know. It's just something men do. They kiss gorgeous women. Every chance they get."

Lame, Nick. Very lame.

Granted, he didn't do it that often. Especially not with women like her.

But a man just snapped every now and then, didn't he?

He was only human.

"I need to do something," she said, putting a hand on the arm of his chair and leaning toward him.

"Do what?" he asked, thinking either he was crazy or she was about to kiss him.

God.

Why?

Just the thought took his breath away.

"I just do," she said, as if that explained everything.

"Why?" he asked.

"Because I need to try to understand," she claimed.

"Understand what?" He leaned back as far as he possibly could in his chair, putting off as long as he could the moment when her mouth settled over his. It was killing him, but he did it.

Because if she actually kissed him, he wasn't sure what he'd do.

"I need to see if it felt as good as I think it did," she said.

That was all she wanted? He laughed. He could tell her that.

"It felt great. I remember. I swear to you, it felt fantastic."

"See, I think it did, too. If I remember correctly. But it shouldn't," she claimed. "Because I'm in love with someone else."

"Oh." That guy. The pirate.

Nick had forgotten all about him when he'd kissed her.

He'd forgotten about everything.

"And if I'm really in love with him, I shouldn't be kissing other men—"

"Of course," Nick said, when she was so close, he could feel her breath fanning his cheek as she slowly exhaled.

He could smell her, too.

That stuff he'd watched her rub all over herself after her bath.

She smelled really good.

"And if I do happen to kiss another man, it shouldn't feel as good as it did to kiss you," she reasoned.

"Okay," Nick said. "Sure."

"So I thought…now that I've had some time to think about

it and now that I'm not so scared, that I need to kiss you again. Just to see how it feels."

Nick nodded. "Like a science experiment."

"Yes. If you don't mind?"

She put her free hand on his cheek, turning his mouth to hers. Her eyes were a dark, deep blue, her touch light as a feather, his senses filled with her.

"Well, if that's what you have to do…"

"Thank you," she whispered, those achingly soft lips settling against his, the barest hint of a taste of her getting to him, hitting his system like a drug, the kind of drug a man craved, a taste he'd do anything for, make any kind of stupid, idiotic mistake to get.

He dug his fingers into the arms of his chair, to keep from grabbing her and pulling her onto his lap, and tried very hard not to move anything else at all, to let her do what she wanted, what she needed to do, without any reaction at all from him.

Yeah, right, Nick finally told himself.

A man would have to be dead not to respond when she kissed him.

He groaned, opened his mouth to hers and thrust deep inside. She gasped, but didn't pull away. Just in case, he grabbed her by the waist and pulled her onto his lap, arms locking around her. Her head fell to his shoulder and soon he had a hand on one very soft, perfectly round breast, his hand slipping inside her shirt, beneath her bra, finding warm, soft skin and a tight little nub of a nipple.

He kissed her like a man who was drowning in her, in the sensations she created in his body. And he couldn't get close enough, devouring her with his mouth, her and those little sounds she made in the back of her throat. Aching sounds. Give-me-more sounds. Take-me-upstairs sounds?

He wished.

Now she groaned, her hand locked in his hair, tugging his face down to the side of her neck and then in the general vicinity of her breasts. At least, that's what he told himself. It was what he hoped, as he nudged her shirt aside with his nose and left kisses along a trail from her collarbone down inside her shirt.

She squirmed on his lap, pressing her pretty bottom against his groin.

His day was complete, his happiness off the charts.

Life was very, very, very good.

He didn't deserve this, but he didn't care.

For the moment, she was his.

His mouth found her nipple, teeth gently nipping. She squirmed even more.

He was such a happy man.

He was thinking of her after her bath, skin all rosy and warm and still a little wet. Thinking of taking her in his arms then, her without a stitch on, and kissing his way down her body and then back up again. Of how sweet she'd smell, how sweet she'd taste, of how she'd look if she was naked and his.

She shuddered in his arms and clung to him, moaned.

Could he strip off her clothes right here?

Just how dark and secluded was the backyard?

He wasn't an exhibitionist, just didn't want to wait long enough to carry her upstairs.

His mouth came back to hers, going deep inside, telling her with his tongue what he wanted to be doing with his body, needing her to understand, to know if she was willing or if he had gone stark-raving mad.

"Nick?" she whispered, breaking off the kiss.

He heard her from very far away, like her voice was coming at him through a thick, billowing fog.

"Nick?"

Louder this time, more insistent.

She was pushing him away, he realized.

He raised his head, opened his eyes. "What?"

"Stop," she said.

"Stop?" He was afraid he sounded like a seventeen-year-old. *Stop? Now? Really?*

"What's wrong?" he asked.

"Everything," she said, sounding sad as could be as she scrambled off his lap and ran inside.

Nick was still breathing hard when she disappeared.

Damn.

Nick told himself he was a man. A strong, determined man. And that she was just a woman. A gorgeous one, but yes, just a woman. And that he could resist.

For the third night in a row since the mysterious sugar-thief incident, she was here in a room right down the hall from him, scared, obviously, because she was still here, but feeling foolish about it after so much time had passed without anything else happening.

Still, they hadn't found anyone who'd had a legitimate reason to be in her apartment that day. She was there a good bit of the time, but late at night, when no one was looking, she crept next door to sleep in the room down the hall from Nick.

If something didn't break soon, she'd go back to her place and Nick would worry even more. Or someone would figure out she was sleeping at the B&B and want an explanation. Like one of her sisters or her brother.

The brother kept running into Nick's men and was suspicious. Any day now, Nick figured the brother would figure out what was going on. Nick didn't want to be around when that happened.

They still hadn't found Eric Weyzinski, although they had a photo of the sugar thief, a man in a phone company uniform, looking away from the camera, a hat obscuring most of his face.

It might or might not be Eric.

They couldn't ask Kim without coming up with some really hard-to-come-up-with explanations and Nick was stuck, not knowing what to do. Kim was right down the hall from him, his landlady probably planted in the hallway between them, obviously curious as could be about what was going on.

Every night, Nick listened while Kim did things in her room, the getting-ready-for-bed things he really didn't want to know about or to imagine. And he sat by that window and looked down into her empty apartment, thankful that she wasn't there, but wishing someone else was, so that this whole thing could be over and he could get out of this town before he did something he'd regret.

Like kiss her again.

Or blow the case by telling her too much.

Or both.

Before he hurt her and became just one more man that she learned she could not trust.

Because he wasn't the man she thought he was and he knew women like her. He wasn't the kind of man a woman like her wanted. A staying kind of guy. A guy who didn't know how to lie the way Nick did. A guy who'd had things in his life that had lasted, relationships that had lasted. A guy who knew how to care about people.

She deserved all that and Nick wasn't the man to give it to her.

It was very, very late before he climbed into bed that night, later still when he finally fell asleep.

He should have known he'd dream of her. Of sinking into sleep, the two of them a tangle of arms and legs, soft, creamy skin, long, blond hair, perfect lips, all of that. Couldn't she even leave him alone while he slept?

He dreamed of finding her in his bed in the middle of the night, her warm, soft body pressed up against his back.

Nick grinned just thinking about it. He snuggled a bit closer, thought about turning over and wrapping his arms around her, but if he was asleep that might be enough to wake him up and he didn't want to wake up.

He wanted to imagine—or maybe he didn't have to imagine—that she was there, sleeping in his bed. That she would wrap her arms around him, warm and willing in sleep. That when he woke up all he'd have to do was turn over and there she'd be. He'd kiss her soft, soft lips, take her into his arms and…

Okay, he really couldn't wait for that to happen.

If he woke up, he woke up and ruined a perfectly good dream.

But if he wasn't asleep and it wasn't a dream, he could be enjoying it a lot more.

He rolled over, an arm coming out to wrap around her, found hair and a little, warm body.

A really little, warm body….

Nick opened his eyes, thinking he still might see her there, that he'd be practically nose to nose with her and could kiss her awake. When he opened his eyes it was still dark, the room nothing but shadows and…

"Aaaarrrrrruuuhhhh!"

He saw what looked like a mouth and lots of teeth, clearly not the woman of his dreams.

"Aaahhhhh!" he roared right back.

Who the hell was in his room?

There was a scramble of movement. He blinked once, then again, hoping to clear his vision.

Was he still asleep?

Was this a nightmare?

Because it was awfully loud for a nightmare.

Instinctively, he grabbed for his gun, which he slept with tucked between the mattress and the box spring, and took aim at the source of the noise.

He heard a crash of some sort, heard what he was sure was Kim scream from down the hall and then something came at him, and he didn't have time to think, just react.

He'd been trained to think first, shoot later, but when someone was coming at you in the dark in a split second, you either put a stop to it or let it get you. That was it. No choice. And if they stopped him, there'd be no one to protect Kim.

He squeezed the trigger, heart pounding, breath ragged, still not completely sure he was awake.

There was an ungodly howl of protest.

Honestly, it didn't even sound human.

What the hell had he hit?

He had hit it, hadn't he?

No way he was lowering his gun until he knew.

"Don't move!" he ordered.

Kim woke in an unfamiliar bed, an unfamiliar room, to the weirdest sounds. She didn't know what they were.

Then she heard a crash coming from Nick's room, and then—oh, God, it sounded like a gunshot. Kim took off running toward him with a baseball bat she'd found tucked away in a closet and stashed by her bed three nights ago, just in case, before she went to sleep. Not that a baseball bat would be that helpful against a gun, but it was the best she could do.

Had that really been a gunshot?

Who would have a gun in Mrs. Baker's B&B?

"Kim?" Mrs. Baker called out. "Are you okay? What was that?"

"I'm not sure," Kim yelled back. "Call 911! Now!"

And then, bat in hand, she charged into Nick's room, ready to do battle, because she couldn't leave him alone, defenseless in his room, against a guy with a gun. She just couldn't.

She pushed the door open, raised the bat, ready to swing and found…

Nick with a gun?

Why would Nick have a gun?

"Don't move!" he ordered.

The gun swung toward her and she screamed, skidded to a halt in her bare feet, still holding the bat.

And then the gun swung back to whatever he'd been aiming at before she came in, which was making an awful, howling noise.

What was it?

"Get the light, Kim," he yelled.

She found the switch and flipped it.

Light flooded the room, blinding her for a moment.

She winced, then blinked twice against the improbable scene before her.

Nick was sitting on the side of his bed, shirtless, a huge, menacing-looking gun firmly in hand and pointed down at the floor where…

The cat, Cleo, was standing, back arched, hair raised,

hissing and scowling at Nick, making a horrible howling noise like nothing Kim had ever heard from the cat before.

And…bleeding?

The cat was bleeding, its front right paw held off the ground. There was a little pool of blood under its right paw.

"You shot the cat?" Kim yelled.

"No, I didn't shoot the cat!" Nick claimed.

"But you shot your gun? That was you?"

"Yeah."

"You have a gun?"

"Yeah, I have a gun."

"And you shot it?"

"Yes, I fired the gun—"

"And the cat's bleeding, but you expect me to believe you didn't shoot it?"

"I wouldn't shoot a cat," he claimed, all evidence to the contrary. "I shot at someone who was in my room, who attacked me."

Kim looked around, not sure what to believe.

She was still half asleep and Nick might be, too. She wasn't absolutely certain she was awake, although why she'd dream of Nick shooting Mrs. Baker's cat, she couldn't imagine.

Cleo was still protesting loudly, and she was standing in the middle of some broken glass, Kim realized.

The cat seemed to realize sympathy was available, if she wanted it, and she decided to plead her case to Kim. Cleo held up her right paw, dripping with blood, to Kim and started meowing pitifully.

"Oh, you poor baby."

Kim dropped the bat and picked up the cat gingerly, fussing over its poor, injured paw. There was a long, angry-looking scrape from halfway down its front leg to its paw, raw and welling with blood. It was definitely no little run-in with a bit of broken glass on the floor.

"You shot the cat!" she yelled at Nick.

"I'm telling you, it's the glass—"

"No, it's not. You don't skid on broken glass and get a gash three inches long. You shot her!"

"There is no way I'd shoot a cat," Nick claimed.

Cleo hissed at him and held up her wounded paw, as if to say, *What do you have to say about this, you jerk?*

"Oh, baby," Kim said, hugging the poor cat closer to her.

She grabbed the closest thing she could find to stop the bleeding, which happened to be Nick's white shirt, and wrapped it around the poor kitty's paw.

"I am so sorry, you sweet thing," Kim crooned. "I can't believe that awful man did this to you."

If it were possible, Kim would have sworn the cat stuck out its bottom lip and started pouting prettily.

"I know," Kim said, then turned to Nick. "Silly, old man—"

"And I am not old!" Nick roared.

Kim shielded the cat as best she could from his outburst, hugging it more tightly and covering one of Cleo's ears with her hand, pressing the other against her shoulder and giving Cleo a kiss on the top of her head. "Don't you worry. I'll take care of you and him."

"What are you going to do?" Nick asked. "Shoot me back?"

"Maybe."

He looked completely baffled. "Where the hell is the guy who was in my room?"

"Did you actually see someone in your room?" she demanded.

"Yes. I think so—"

"And how's your eyesight, Nick?"

"My eyesight is just fine, dammit—"

She was mad enough to add, "Night vision? How about that? I hear it gets worse with age."

"Oh, that was low," he complained.

"Not as low as shooting a cat!"

"Okay, I might have grazed the damned cat," he admitted. "Maybe. I don't see how, but…maybe."

"Maybe you should look before you start shooting. And why do you have a gun, anyway?"

"I always have a gun," he told her, then looked like he wished he hadn't.

From downstairs, Mrs. Baker yelled, "I've got 911 on the phone. They want to know what our emergency is. I wasn't sure what to tell them."

"911?" Nick looked at her accusingly. "You told her to call 911?"

"Yes, I told her to call 911. It's the middle of the night, I hear a gunshot down the hall from where I'm sleeping and I want someone to call 911. I'm funny that way."

"Dammit," he swore softly, then yelled, "We're fine, Mrs. Baker. Just a little misunderstanding."

"Misunderstanding?" Kim couldn't believe him.

"Yes, a misunderstanding," he whispered urgently. "The cat knocked a glass off the nightstand and broke it," he yelled.

"That was a glass breaking? I thought I heard a gunshot?"

"Two glasses," Nick claimed, lying through his teeth.

Lying rather well, Kim noticed.

"Back me up," he insisted, still holding the gun, she realized.

Not pointed at her or the cat or anything in particular, but still holding it.

She looked from him, to the gun, then back to him again.

He glanced down at his hand, at the gun, then back at her. “You’ve got to be kidding me. You think I’m going to hurt you?”

“I don’t know,” she said. “You have a gun and you shot the cat.”

Chapter Ten

Kim's brother would have told her to hang on to the cat and run or scream or throw something, anything but just stand there and talk to a man she didn't really know that well who had a gun in his hand in the middle of the night, a gun he'd already fired.

Nick swore long and none too quietly, then put the gun down on the nightstand and held up his empty hands for her to see.

"No more gun. Now, will you please tell Mrs. Baker to tell the nice 911 dispatcher that we don't need any help here, that it was all a misunderstanding, and then tell her to go back to bed, that we're all fine."

"Why should I?" Kim asked.

"Because I don't want to have to explain to anyone why I'm here, why I have a gun and why I shot a cat, thinking it was someone in my room, coming to get me, so they could get to you."

"Get to me? Why would anyone with a gun want to come and get me?"

"Kim—" he began.

"Kim?" Mrs. Baker yelled. "Should I come up there and—"

"No, don't come up here," Kim said.

That was the last thing they needed.

"Tell her everything's okay. You and I will take care of the cat and I'll explain everything to you," Nick claimed.

"Everything?"

"Yes, everything."

She didn't quite see how he could, how it could possibly make sense. He'd shot the cat!

What kind of man shot a cat!

"Kim?" Mrs. Baker called out again.

"We're fine, Mrs. Baker. Everything's under control. Tell them it was a misunderstanding."

"Thank you," Nick said.

Cleo hissed at him once more and Kim felt like doing the same thing.

"I don't trust you," she said instead. "Not really."

"Fine. Don't trust me. Just don't rat me out yet. This isn't what you think."

"I don't know how it could not be what I think, when I have no earthly idea what I think right now," she protested.

"Okay. Fine. But I can explain everything. Really, I can."

Cleo didn't seem to be in the mood for any explanations Nick might make. She hissed at him again, then leaped out of Kim's arms, lost the shirt that had been wrapped around her grazed leg and landed on the pretty, tangled white sheets and the old-fashioned quilt on Nick's bed.

She tiptoed daintily across them, leaving little bloody paw prints as she went.

"Cleo, no," Kim said.

The quilt was likely an antique. How would they explain bloody paw prints all over Mrs. Baker's quilt?

Nick went to grab the cat and Cleo bit him on the arm with a roar that said, *Take that, you cat shooter, you!*

"Dammit," Nick said again, grabbing his now-bleeding forearm. "That cat is vicious!"

"Only to people who shoot her first," Kim said.

"It was a scratch," Nick protested. "A little scratch."

Cleo leaped from the bed to Nick's suitcase, which was standing open on a luggage stand in the corner, and before Nick could get to her, the cat—looking extremely pleased with herself—started marching around, bloody paw and all, on Nick's crisp, white shirts, on his socks, his tightie-whities and anything else the cat could find, a look of pure, absolute, vindictive glee on her face as she did it.

Nick, holding his bleeding forearm, said, "Would you get it off my clothes while I might still have something to wear without blood stains on it."

Kim went to do just that, but only because she wanted him to have a shirt to put on. The sight of him in nothing but a thin pair of pajama bottoms was something she really didn't need right now. It was making it hard for her to think and she needed to think.

Cleo, unfortunately, didn't want Nick to have anything to wear. She growled at him, dodged Kim when she tried to get her off Nick's clothes, then launched herself at Nick, landing somewhere in the vicinity of his lap, claws extended and digging in.

Nick sucked in a breath, his abdomen going concave as he tried to get away from the cat's claws. He gasped, then made a pitiful, howling sound, not that unlike the one Cleo had been making.

Cleo was gone before he had a chance to swat her away, gone into the shelter of Kim's arms, snuggling close and looking indignant and wounded once again.

Blood welled up from angry-looking scratches low on Nick's tanned, taut abdomen and maybe from a few other places, a little lower down, that Kim did not want to think about.

Served him right, shooting a poor, sweet thing like Cleo.

Kim kissed the cat's head and said, "Poor baby. You showed him, didn't you?"

"I've run into some problems when I've been traveling," Nick said for maybe the third time in the last twenty minutes.

"You? A parks planner?" Kim wasn't buying it.

"Yes. You think parks planners are magically immune to the craziness in the world these days? You think anyone is? I mean, you just got shot at by pirates, after all."

"Yeah, but I'm not living with a loaded gun under my pillow."

"Well, maybe you should," Nick said. "And I don't keep it under my pillow. I keep it between the mattress and the box spring."

"I don't care where you keep it. I care that you have it and that you shot the cat," Kim said.

They were in Nick's little red midlife-crisis car, zooming toward the outskirts of Atlanta and the emergency vet's, because Kim had insisted and because there was no way she was going to try to clean the cat's scrapes by herself. Not after seeing what Cleo's claws had done to Nick. And maybe because it was one thing Kim knew that had to get done—taking care of the cat. It was simple and fairly easy and none of the other things that needed to happen would be simple or easy.

She had to figure out what was going on here, and she wasn't sure she wanted to know. Although before they'd snuck out of Mrs. Baker's house in the predawn hours, she'd grabbed a tiny can of mace from her bedroom, just in case. She'd brought it with her the first night she'd spent at Mrs. Baker's, never thinking she might need to use it against Nick. And she'd gotten a friend out of bed and told her if she didn't hear from her within the hour to call Kim's brother and tell him she might have been kidnapped by a supposedly mild-mannered parks planner in a little red sports car, then gave her friend the license plate number, just in case.

A woman couldn't be too careful these days.

She didn't have to get in a car with guys who slept with guns and shot cats, but…dammit. Kim didn't know what to think as she sat in the car beside Nick, zooming along toward the emergency vet. She figured if he was really going to kidnap her, they wouldn't have brought the cat along, because Nick was still complaining about how much cat scratches hurt and maybe because it was all the reassurance she could offer herself.

Maybe she really was a first-class idiot where men were concerned, Nick and the supposed love of her life included.

Nick looked like he'd been on the losing end of a fight with a woman who had fingernails from hell. He'd pulled on his pants with a frightening degree of difficulty. Kim didn't want to think about where Cleo's claws might have landed other than his forearm and abdomen. But he had streaks of blood that had stained his shirtsleeve and the front right lower section of his shirt.

His room looked like someone had committed a massacre in it and it had been a miracle they'd managed to talk Mrs. Baker out of having the 911 dispatcher send the cops over and going into Nick's room, then managed to sneak out of the house with her cat for a trip to the emergency vet.

Cleo was curled up in Kim's lap, protesting here and there as they drove, still glaring at Nick every now and then.

Kim thought Nick was actually scared of the cat, too, which she felt he fully deserved.

And she wasn't buying his story for one minute.

"Well, sorry, but if someone had broken in, you'd have been glad I had a gun," he claimed.

"Oh, yeah. You could have taken out a bird or the neighbor's dog, you're such a good shot and all. Do you even know how to use that thing? I mean, it's not a toy—"

"Yes, I know how to use it—"

"People with a gun in their home are much more likely to injure themselves or have one of their family members injured by the gun than to actually shoot an intruder. If you'd read the statistics, you'd know—"

"I know the damned statistics. I know how to use the gun," he claimed.

Cleo growled at him. She was proving to be a wonderfully vindictive cat, with good reason, Kim thought. Nick had better watch his back. And just about every other part of himself.

"Look, I heard a crash, breaking glass and then something hurled itself at me in the dark when I wasn't quite awake and, granted, it wasn't the smartest thing to do—to shoot at anything unless I was absolutely sure what I was shooting at—"

"Gun Safety 101. Don't shoot unless you know—"

"But sometimes, you don't have time to ask questions, you know? It's you or whoever's coming at you—"

"Or an innocent cat—"

"It is not innocent!" he yelled. "What the hell was it doing in my room anyway? I was sound asleep in my room, minding my own business, when that thing attacked me for no reason—"

"She attacked you?"

"Yes, she did—"

"She probably just wanted to get in bed with you. She's a very affectionate cat. And the room you're sleeping in used to belong to Mrs. Baker's daughter, Dana. I think Cleo used to sleep with her. So technically, you're in the cat's bed, not the other way around."

"How did she even get in?"

"She's very good with doors. She can open anything."

"Great," Nick said. "I'll have to barricade my door against an attack cat."

"If Mrs. Baker even lets you stay, once she finds out what you did."

Nick glared at her and the cat, who hissed at him once more and bared her teeth to him.

Kim stroked the cat and wondered what kind of damage Cleo could do if she really sank her teeth into someone, not unsure Nick shouldn't find out. She didn't believe him for a minute about why he had the gun and what kind of man, when he wakes up in the middle of the night because of a noise, grabs a gun, shoots first and asks questions later.

Not any men she knew.

Her brother wouldn't think of doing something like that. In all his years on the job, he'd only fired his weapon once. People who knew guns fired at the practice range and hardly anywhere else at any point in their lives.

So what was Nick Cavanaugh doing with a gun? And why would he shoot first and ask questions later?

She didn't like guns. She'd been shot at on the cruise ship by pirates and now she'd had someone fire a gun at a cat in the B&B in the middle of the night, right down the hall from her room. This after going her whole life without being shot at.

It was too strange a coincidence to ignore.

And yet, what could Nick possibly have to do with the pirates who attacked her cruise ship? How could one possibly be connected to the other?

She wanted her brother, the cop. Kind of.

Actually, she wanted her mother, but her brother would do. He was every bit as protective as a mother and he carried a gun and, unlike Nick, knew how to use it.

Her brother was good at figuring things out, too. He'd never met a fellow law-enforcement officer he didn't remember and couldn't call on when he needed help.

Kind of like Nick's friend at the phone company, she decided.

If the guy really worked at the phone company….

She was just starting to get a very bad feeling about that…the phone company guy of Nick's and how he seemed to be able to get information on just about anything, when they pulled into the emergency vet's around five o'clock in the morning.

She got out of the car, gently cradling the cat, and glanced over at Nick and his bloodstained shirt.

"You'd better let me go in first," Kim said. "You're likely to scare them."

"You've got blood on your shirt, too," he pointed out.

Indeed, she did, but not as much as him, and the blood on her shirt was mostly covered up by the cat she was carrying.

They marched in together to an insanely brightly lit room bustling with activity. Cleo went on alert immediately, thanks to the two tiny barking dogs in the waiting room. Kim felt claws sinking into her arms and felt a tad of sympathy for Nick. Just a tad.

She tried to reassure Cleo that everything was going to be okay, while Nick gave some outlandish explanation about Cleo's injuries—broken glass, he claimed—to the skeptical receptionist, who was eyeing Nick's bloody shirt with some degree of cynicism, but at least not with alarm. Maybe lots of people showed up bloody at the emergency vet's.

"It's a hundred and fifty dollars for an office visit," the receptionist said.

"A hundred and fifty dollars?" Nick said incredulously.

The receptionist nodded.

"For a cat?"

"At five in the morning, yes," the receptionist said. "Part of the cost of having emergency care available round the clock—nights, weekends and holidays."

"That's fine," Kim said. "He'll pay."

"In more ways than one," Nick muttered, reaching for his wallet.

The receptionist showed them to a private room a few moments later and gave them a ton of paperwork to fill out, none of which Nick could do. He knew nothing about the cat. He passed the clipboard and the forms over to Kim.

The vet technician arrived moments later, frowning at both the explanation she received and what she could see of the cat's injuries.

"The cat's pretty riled up. We may have to sedate her to even get a good look at the wound," the vet tech said.

"That's fine. Do it," Nick said.

"It makes it more expensive—"

"We don't care. Just do it," Nick said.

"I mean, we usually have to see the wound before we can even give you an estimate and you have to approve the treatment and the costs before we actually treat the cat, so—"

"Money is no object," Nick said, pulling out his wallet again and looking at Kim. "Right, honey?"

"That's right, dear," she said, giving him a fake smile.

"I have a feeling I'm going to be paying for this for a long time and not just with money," he told the vet tech, then whispered into Kim's ear. "I'm not sure, but I may never be able to father children, thanks to that cat."

"What a pity," Kim said.

They ended up spending three hours at the emergency vet's. The wound wasn't all that bad. Just a scrape really, Kim had to admit, not that deep but long and painful. When they examined Cleo, they found several teeth that the vet felt needed to come out—an infection risk, he said, as cats got older, made worse by the wound, but still, something their regular vet could take care of in the next few days.

"Since you're going to have her sedated anyway, why don't you go ahead and pull them," Kim said with a great deal of satisfaction.

The vet looked puzzled. "It would cost a lot less if your regular vet did it. Our fees aren't cheap."

"I know, but it's fine. Nick will pay," Kim said. She smiled up at him. "Might as well get everything taken care of while we're here, right honey?"

Nick gritted his teeth and smiled and reached for his credit card again.

"How did you say this happened?" the vet asked one more time.

"Broken glass," Nick claimed. "The cat jumped through a window, scraped its paw on the way out."

The vet frowned, obviously not convinced. "Because I've never seen a broken-glass wound quite like this."

"Really?" Nick feigned innocence so well it was frightening.

"It looks more like a gunshot wound," the vet said.

"Why would anyone shoot a cat?" Mr. Innocent asked.

Kim rolled her eyes at that, and Nick elbowed her, as if to say, *Back me up here, would you please?*

"But she is going to be okay, isn't she?" Kim asked.

"Sure. You just need to watch out for infection, that's all."

"We will," Kim promised. "Won't we, Nickie?"

"I'm not going anywhere near the cat and the cat had better not come anywhere near me," he muttered, then excused himself to go take a phone call.

Kim smiled up at the vet, a model-slim pretty brunette close to six feet tall. "He and Cleo are still getting to know each other, but I'm sure they'll be able to come to terms."

The bill ended up being a thousand dollars.

Kim was extremely pleased.

"Mrs. Baker was saving up the money to have the teeth taken care of, but with all the expenses of opening the B&B, it would have been a while, and…well, you deserve to pay," Kim said as they climbed into Nick's car with a sleepy, still half-sedated cat.

"Fine. I'll just have to find a way to explain it on my expense account," he said.

"I'm sure you'll be very creative. After all, you're a great liar—"

"Kim, I couldn't tell the vet—"

"It's not about the vet. It's about you and everything you've told me—"

"What do you think it is I've told you that wasn't true?"

"Oh, I don't know….everything? If you're a parks planner, I'm Miss America—"

"I'm sure you could be, if that's what you wanted—"

"And don't be nice to me. Not now. I'm not in the mood, and it's not going to work."

"Okay. Okay," he said.

"Okay, you'll tell me everything?"

"Yeah. Okay," he said, grim-faced and looking…

She couldn't quite say how he looked.

Different.

Completely different.

More serious, completely capable, not nearly as nice and understanding as he'd been, like a man who didn't have a gentle bone in his body, although when she'd been in his arms, she'd have sworn he did.

He'd been extremely gentle with her. Hungry for her, no mistaking that. Her heartbeat kicked up a notch just thinking about it, about the things he'd done to her and how it had felt. About the way she'd gone so willingly into his arms, telling herself she just had to do it a second time to see if it had really felt as great as she feared.

And she'd been right.

It had been great.

Fabulous.

Thrilling.

Everything, she decided.

Everything a woman wanted to feel with a man.

And in a way she couldn't begin to explain or understand, so much more than she'd felt with the man she was supposed to be in love with, the one who seemed to have abandoned her without another thought, for reasons she would probably never understand.

She'd made a mistake, a big one, in falling for Eric and thinking she was in love with him and telling everyone about it. She felt so foolish for that, so naive, so stupid. But she had a sad feeling that the bigger mistake was believing everything Nick Cavanaugh had to say. Trusting him. Going along with him and a half-dozen suggestions he had made.

Kissing him.

Liking it so much.

Even falling for him a little along the way.

She felt so incredibly stupid.

"Do we have to do this now? On the road?" he asked when she wasn't saying anything. "Or can it wait until we get back to town?"

"I guess it can wait that long," she said, trying to extract a promise from herself not to cry all over him.

That would be the ultimate humiliation.

"Just tell me one thing," she said.

"Okay."

"Does this have something to do with Eric?"

Nick nodded.

"He's not who I thought he was, is he?"

"No."

She nodded.

Okay.

There it was.

She'd been a fool.

She took a breath, a shaky one, a weak I'm-not-going-to-cry hiccupy breath and hated herself just a little bit more.

"And you're not at all who I thought you were, either, right?" she asked.

"No, Kim, I'm not."

Chapter Eleven

They got back to the B&B that morning to find a worried-looking Mrs. Baker on the porch.

Kim had left her a vague note about leaving early with Nick on an errand, not to worry, that they'd be back soon. She was waiting for them when they pulled to the curb in front of the B&B, a still-sleepy, well-medicated Cleo curled up in Kim's arms.

Mrs. Baker gasped at the bloody clothes, as Kim explained, kind of, what had happened and that they'd taken Cleo to the vet, but she hadn't needed stitches, just a big bandage and some antibiotic ointment. She wasn't quite sure how to explain the teeth coming out at Nick's expense, so she didn't even try at the moment. For now, the cat was fine.

"I'm so sorry for all the trouble. I should have warned you that she thinks the bed you're in is really hers," Mrs. Baker told Nick, the sleepy cat now in her arms.

"Don't be silly. It was all Nick's fault," Kim said.

"It was?" Mrs. Baker looked confused.

"It was," Kim said and didn't try to explain that, either. She was starting to realize that maybe she didn't have to explain everything to everyone and it suited her at the moment not to, so she didn't.

"All right," Mrs. Baker said, confusion evident. "Well, I should pay you for the vet visit—"

"Nick paid," Kim told her. "He insisted."

"Oh. Well…thank you, Nick."

"You're welcome," he said.

"I…uh…tried to get into your room, Nick, to clean up the mess, but the door seems to be jammed or something…."

Nick nodded. "I didn't want you to have to clean it up. I fix my own messes."

"Oh… Okay," Mrs. Baker said. "If you insist."

"He does," Kim said, taking him by the arm. "Come on, Nick. I'll help you clean up your mess."

"Oh." Mrs. Baker stood there, puzzled, as they walked away. "Okay. Well…I was going to the grocery store. I have to pick up some things. But maybe I should wait. Poor Cleo…"

"She'll be fine and the vet said she'll probably sleep for hours," Kim said, turning around and taking the cat from Mrs. Baker. "I'll take her inside and put her in her favorite spot on the sofa by the front window."

"Well…okay."

"Don't worry about anything. We'll all be fine," Kim called out over her shoulder as they marched inside.

"Will I be fine?" Nick asked.

"Shut up," Kim told him, dropping his arm the minute they got into the house and away from Mrs. Baker's prying eyes.

For a moment out there, mild-mannered Nick, the parks

planner, had been back, nonthreatening and almost ordinary as could be. It had been truly unsettling and a little scary to see how easily he made the transformation from the man she'd known to the one she'd discovered with a gun in his hand, aimed at her and the cat, the night before.

She truly didn't know him.

She put Cleo down on the sofa, fussed over her for a moment and told her what a good kitty she was and that she could sleep the day away if she wanted to.

Mrs. Baker stuck her head in the front door and said, "Kim, I forgot. Gwen brought the dogs over. She said you needed them for something? Some kind of art project?"

"Yes, I do," Kim said.

"They're in the backyard."

"Thank you, Mrs. Baker."

She left once again.

"Dogs?" Nick asked. "What are we doing with dogs?"

"You'll see," Kim said.

He followed her to the back door and outside, where a beautiful tan-colored Australian shepherd and a little white fur ball were curled up together in the shade under an oak tree. They scrambled to their feet and barked out a greeting as they spotted Kim and headed for her.

Nick backed up a step and made a face.

She got down on her knees and greeted the dogs, fussing over them one by one and telling them how much she missed them, how glad she was that they'd come to visit.

"This is Nick," she told them. "He's a jerk."

The dogs cocked their heads to the side, as if trying to discern the meaning of the word jerk.

"Kim—"

"This is Romeo and this is Petunia."

Nick frowned. “Am I supposed to shake their hands or something?”

“Only if you want yours taken off in one bite. Romeo was my mother’s dog. He’s police-academy trained. You don’t want to mess with him. I say *Bite* and he says *How hard?* And he doesn’t often get to attack people, so he usually does it with great enthusiasm.”

“Okay. What’s the other one here for? The flower-dog?”

Romeo growled at Nick, as if he got that insult completely.

“She’s my sister-in-law’s dog and the love of Romeo’s life. She goes everywhere he goes.”

“Okay, but really, Petunia?”

“My sister-in-law found her abandoned behind a flower shop. Don’t make fun of her. Romeo doesn’t like it, right Romeo?”

He growled again, right on cue.

“Good dog,” Kim said. “Let’s go inside and get this over with.”

“Get what over with?” Nick asked.

“Your lame-ass explanation.”

“It’s not lame,” he said.

Kim didn’t bother to stay and argue. She went inside, calling the dogs to follow her. They trailed after her upstairs and to the door of Nick’s room, which Kim couldn’t open either.

“What did you do to it?” she asked, as Nick came to stand beside her by the door.

“Just jimmied the lock. I was afraid if Mrs. Baker saw all the blood, she’d have a heart attack.”

He did something to the lock that Kim couldn’t see and, within seconds, they were in.

The dogs must have smelled the blood, because they went instantly on alert, Romeo growling and sniffing his way around the room.

"No dead bodies, I promise," Nick said.

Romeo snarled at him and Nick backed up.

"Okay," Nick said, then turned to Kim. "You're afraid of me now?"

"I'm being smart, that's all."

She'd called her sister-in-law from the all-night vet's and asked her to bring over the dogs, just in case. Now that she was alone with Nick in his room, she pulled her can of mace out of her purse.

Pointing the mace at him, she said, "Go ahead. I'm ready."

He shook his head and swore softly into the air.

Kim took a seat by the window then told the dogs to sit by the foot of the bed, so they wouldn't get near the broken glass left on the floor on the other side of the room. She was ready for this and she was not going to cry. She was going to find out who this man was and what he was doing here and then she was going to deal with it, whatever the problem was.

She was not going to be stupid anymore.

"All right," she told Nick. "Tell me. Everything. What are you doing here? Start with that?"

"I've been following you," he admitted as he stood by the chest of drawers against the side wall, standing straight and tall, looking incredibly alert, completely in control for someone who'd hardly gotten any sleep.

It was so irritating, she wanted to throw something at him.

"Why are you following me?" she asked.

"Because you're one of the few links we have to Eric Weyzinski."

Kim took a breath. She could handle this. "And Eric Weyzinski is—"

"The jerk who seduced you on the ship."

Her face flamed at the word *seduced* and all it entailed.

"You've been following me since I got back from the cruise?" she asked.

"No, Kim. From the time you were on the ship. We were on the ship, too. We saw the whole thing go down."

"Go down? You mean, the attack?"

Nick nodded.

"Eric saved me from them," she insisted. "He shoved me down when they started firing and shielded me with his own body."

"Which made him look like he had nothing to do with the attack. Yeah, we know. We were there."

"You keep saying, *We*. Who's *We?*"

"I'm with a hush-hush division of Homeland Security. A counterterrorism agency."

"Agency?" Her mouth gaped open. "You're some kind of secret agent?"

He nodded once again, maddeningly calm while he told the most outlandish tale.

She had befriended him, worried over him, laughed with him, kissed him more than once and there he stood, telling her he was a spy, living next door to her in Mrs. Baker's B&B?

"I would really like to smack you right now," she said.

"Wouldn't be the first time," he said, shaking his head.

Kim closed her eyes, thinking of what he'd already told her and what she still didn't know. "What did Eric do?"

"We're not sure. We thought at first that he was part of the pirate's attack. That they'd planted someone on the ship to help them get aboard and when they couldn't, he had orders not to blow his cover, so they could try again with another ship at another time—"

"Wait. Pirates? What's up with the pirates? I mean, how can there be pirates in the twenty-first century?"

"There are people ready to rob other people everywhere, always have been and always will be. Including people on boats. And the water's good for them. It's not like you can call 911 and have the cops show up in ten minutes when you're on the water."

"So, it's just about money?" she asked.

"At first. And then the pirates became better organized, better armed, started working together in bigger groups. It was only a matter of time before one of them got the grand idea to knock off a cruise ship. The cruise lines have been training to handle something like this for years."

Kim was horrified. "Who knew? I never knew. I never imagined."

"Not many people did. Don't feel bad about that."

"So, the attack on my ship…? You don't think that was just about money?"

He shrugged. "Like I said, the groups are getting bigger, better armed. It's not hard to imagine someone taking over a ship for other reasons."

"Like…terrorism?"

Nick nodded.

"That's why you were there, watching my ship?"

"We picked up some chatter about a possible move against the ship. That's why we were there."

"And you stopped the attack?"

"We helped," he said.

"But the pirates got away. You were there and you didn't catch them?"

"Not exactly. Sorry, I can't talk about this part of it with you. We're still… We're not done, Kim. We didn't just let them get away."

"Okay." She took a breath, tried to take it all in. She might have been caught up in a terrorist attack. As bad as she felt right now, things could have definitely been worse. "What about Eric? You think he's a terrorist? You think I'm involved with a terrorist?"

"I don't know," he said, staring at her.

"I am not a terrorist!" she cried.

"I know that," he said, finally losing the stone-face that she hated, being exasperated as the Nick she'd known so often was.

"Okay, then that means…I'm just stupid and have no idea who I'm involved with," she said, very near tears. "A stupid, stupid woman."

Romeo lifted his head and whined at her, obviously worried.

She patted his head and he gave her a look that said, *You're upset? I'm sorry. I still love you.*

And she only wanted to cry more.

"I love you, too," she said.

"What?" Nick bellowed.

"I'm talking to the dog!" she said, contemplating her own foolishness.

She'd been an absolute fool.

And everyone in town was going to know about it sooner or later, except for the dogs, who'd love her anyway, thank goodness.

But still, she was an idiot of gigantic proportions, she realized, face flaming.

She'd fancied herself in love with a terrorist!

"He's a con man, Kim. This is what he does for a living. He convinces people he's someone else, someone quite different than who he really is. His success depends on how good he is at putting up a front, so you can imagine he works hard at it. He's had years of practice. He's very, very good at it. It's hard for people like me—people trained to spot criminals—to figure out who the bad guys are at times. People like you—"

"Stupid women—?"

"Normal people—nice, law-abiding people—don't stand much of a chance if somebody like me can't even figure out who the bad guys are."

She gave up and started to cry. There was no more holding back, nothing she could do.

Romeo whined and batted at her side with his head, comforting her as best he could; Petunia crawled into her lap and snuggled against her. They really were the sweetest things.

Kim wrapped her arms around Petunia and let Romeo give her a little kiss. Dogs truly didn't care if their people were stupid. They loved their people anyway. Even stupid people could get lavish, enduring love from dogs.

She should give up on men altogether and go run a kennel or something.

Kim sat there, miserable as could be, sniffling and taking what comfort she could from the dogs. Nick stood like a statue across the room from her, grim-faced and angry.

"I'm sorry," she said, impatient with herself and hating that he got to see her this way. It was humiliating enough to believe herself in love with a terrorist, but to let him see her falling apart this way only made it worse.

"No, I'm sorry. Sorry he ever got near you. Sorry that people like him exist in this world, and sorry that I haven't caught him and locked him up, so he can't terrorize women like you—"

"Women who don't know any better," she said.

"No, that is not what I meant."

Kim buried her face in Petunia's fur and a worried Romeo tried to lick her tears away.

Some vicious watchdog he made.

She was losing any chance she had to convince Nick to be afraid of the dog.

Not that she needed him to be afraid of the dog anymore.

She believed him about everything.

He was a government agent, tailing her, waiting for her criminal of a boyfriend to show up.

Kim shook her head miserably, unable to see how her life had come to this.

She sniffled, determined to stop crying, to understand exactly what she'd gotten into, so it never, ever happened again.

"Eric," she said. "Tell me about Eric. I need to know. He's really a terrorist?"

"We're not sure. He's stolen things in the past. Granted, nothing as big as this, but he's a thief, all right. And there are some vague links between him and suspected terrorists. The whole pirate attack might have been a diversion—"

"A diversion? For what?"

"A theft. One of the calls I took at the vet's office was to tell me that someone on that ship was carrying ten million dollars in diamonds—"

"I didn't hear anything about ten million dollars in diamonds being stolen."

"Well, if you're in the money-laundering business and someone steals your stuff, you don't exactly call the police and report the theft," Nick said.

"Oh. Okay. So…why would they have that much in diamonds on board a cruise ship?"

"We're pretty sure it was a money-laundering operation. That someone got wind of the fact that all those diamonds would be aboard and went after them. Maybe with the pirate attack. Maybe they were supposed to take the diamonds with them as part of their haul from the ship and they never intended on taking hostages and doing who knows what to the people on board. Who knows. We were there. The ship was better prepared to defend itself than they expected. Maybe Eric was there to help them board the ship and when he saw that they weren't going to be able to, he tried to look like the hero by saving you, to keep anyone from being suspicious of him. Or maybe that was part of the backup plan. That in the confusion after the attack, Eric might be able to get to the diamonds himself or that someone else he was working with on the ship could get the diamonds and, if they did, Eric would have to have a way to get the diamonds off the ship without being discovered. Which is where you came into it."

"I didn't help him smuggle ten million dollars in diamonds off the ship," Kim insisted.

"I don't think you did. At least, not knowingly," Nick said, maddeningly calm.

Kim nodded. Great. She was either aiding and abetting terrorists or just plain old diamond thieves.

"So, at best, he's just a thief," she said. "The love of my life, a thief."

"Maybe," Nick said.

"What do you mean, maybe? You just said you think he stole the diamonds."

"Yes."

"So why are you even in this if it's just a theft? Don't you have some other super-secret spy stuff to do? Shouldn't you have packed your bags and left, Mr. Parks Planner?"

He took a breath and let it out slow. "Think about it, Kim. What's he going to do with ten million dollars in diamonds? Terrorists need money. Lots of money to carry out their operations."

"Oh, God. We're back to him being a terrorist and a thief. It sounded so much better, just thinking he was a thief. This is what my life has come to. My boyfriend, under the best possible scenarios, might only be a thief. To think I was hopeful it would only be that. But no, it's even worse. Boyfriend/terrorist/thief."

Kim's brother was going to absolutely flip out. She wouldn't hear the end of this for years. If she thought he watched out for her now, he'd be smothering her in the future. Her sisters wouldn't take it much better. It was bad enough being the baby of the family. But being the youngest and showing that you have absolutely no sense in matters of love and deception…

"This is…I can't even say how awful this is. It's hard to take it all in. The sheer magnitude of the awfulness of it is stunning."

"I know. I'm sorry. So sorry he dragged you into this. And I'm sorry I had to lie to you."

She shook her head, shrugged her shoulders, trying not to care. "It's your job, right? You probably lie to people all the time. And you're very, very good at it."

She looked him right in the eye as she said it and he looked away, tight-lipped once again.

And she'd kissed him. She could have withered up and died right there, just thinking of it. It made her wish she could shrink down to a little ball and then dissolve right before his eyes, never having to face him again.

Yes, she'd kissed him.

More than once.

And really, really liked it.

All the while, supposedly being in love with a terrorist.

Which made her feel even more stupid, if that were possible.

It probably it was.

In love with a terrorist, kissing the secret agent next door.

A double whammy in the striking-out-at-love arena. A real crash-and-burn scenario times two.

"I really hated lying to you, Kim. I swear I did."

She nodded, not sure she was more the fool for wanting to believe him or for hoping what he said was true. That he had found it difficult to lie to her and that maybe she wasn't the most gullible person on earth.

"I've never really been in love before," she said softly. "I mean…obviously, I still haven't. I just meant…I've never felt like that before. I'm not one of those women who runs around falling in love every other day with every guy I meet. I'm careful, and I always thought I was sensible, but now…I guess I'm not."

"They were unusual circumstances," Nick said. "You were in the middle of the Mediterranean Sea on a cruise ship. A gorgeous spot. And you were on vacation. Tons of people think they've fallen in love on vacation. And then you were in the middle of a really dangerous event. Two people thrown together in the middle of a dangerous event. I can't tell you how many times I've seen people fall for each other at times like that. Danger heightens all the senses. Everything seems more intense, every feeling you have. And you thought he'd saved your life. Another out-of-the-ordinary thing that tends to make people feel a lot of things that they don't normally feel. And like I said, the guy's a professional. Fooling people, manipulating them, that's his business."

She nodded, tears falling again. "And he looked at me and said, 'I'll get that one. She looks like she'd be easy to convince that—'"

"He looked at you and thought you were one of the most beautiful women he'd ever seen and he wanted you."

Kim wiped away tears with the back of her hand and tried to smile. "I don't think so. I think he decided he could talk me into anything and he did. I fell for his act completely."

She sniffled, told herself she was pathetic to be wanting

another man who'd also lied to her and whom she'd believed completely, that she wasn't such a fool for believing everything the first one said.

She got to her feet. The dogs scrambled up, as well, giving her worried looks, Romeo growling a bit in Nick's direction.

"It's okay," she told the dog. "We're going to my place. We'll go drown our sorrows in ice cream and doggie treats. It'll be great. And I've heard the grocery store is carrying an ice cream doggie treat, right there in the freezer section by the regular ice cream. Maybe we'll go get some of that, too, because you guys are just the best."

She faced Nick, as dry-eyed as she could manage, and felt her cheeks flame with the heat of utter embarrassment and humiliation. "I'm sorry I…did whatever I did to help him, that I made this an even bigger mess than it already was."

"It's okay. It's not your fault," he said.

"No, it was."

"Kim, we all make mistakes. I mean…I shot a cat, for God's sake. I'm never going to live that one down."

She nodded. "I'm going to go."

But when she brushed past him as she headed for the door, he caught her with a hand on her arm, his worried eyes staring down into hers. "Are you going to be okay?"

She shrugged. "Sure. I mean…people get their hearts broken all the time. They do stupid things and get over them and get on with their lives. Could have been worse, right? It's not like he really hurt me."

"He did hurt you. I know he did. I could take him apart with my bare hands for that alone."

"Thank you," she whispered, telling herself not to do anything else that was stupid.

Like think it meant something, the way he was looking at

her now, those deep, brown eyes full of concern and kindness and maybe something else.

What did she know after all?

She'd fallen for a terrorist.

She was a woman who was clearly not mentally equipped to make valid judgments about any man or any relationship she might have with a man. There must be something lacking somewhere inside her brain, the little gene that handled decisions about men. Hers had obviously mutated into some poor semblance of what it was supposed to be.

Kim could imagine, years from now, some scientist, after spending years locked up in a lab—where she couldn't make any stupid mistakes about men—discovering the genetic mutation responsible for the I-can't-make-good-decisions-about-men disease. There would be gene therapy for it, support groups, telethons and maybe a smidgeon of understanding from all the women whose men-decision genes weren't messed up, and she and other women like her wouldn't feel so lousy about themselves.

But until then…what was there to do?

Stay away from men, Kim decided.

Including the one at her side right now.

The one who seemed both alike and very different from the man she'd thought she'd known. Tougher, stronger, more determined, more capable, altogether more interesting.

"I'm going to lock myself in my bedroom with the dogs," she said.

It seemed like the only place she'd feel safe.

"Okay," Nick said.

"You'll… There's… It's okay? I mean…I'll be okay over there? If Eric shows up, you'll catch him?"

"We'll catch him," Nick promised.

"Okay," she said. "And...well, I'll help you. Any way I can."

"You will?"

She nodded. It was the least she could do.

"I don't want him here. Everyone who's important to me in the world is here. Everyone I love. And I can't just sit back and let him come here and do...whatever he's going to do. You have to stop him and I'm going to help you, before he hurts anyone else."

"Okay," he said.

"Just...tell me what to do. Or figure out what I can do and I'll do it."

"Did he give you anything on the ship? Any little gift?"

"No," she said.

"Ask you to hang on to anything for him?"

"No. Nothing."

Nick swore softly, shaking his head. "What about the things you brought back? Have you unpacked everything? Looked through it completely?"

"Yes. Of course."

"And there's nothing that looks different or unusual? Nothing you don't recognize?"

"No."

"What about gifts you brought back for your family and friends. You did that, right?"

"Yes," she said. "Perfume for my sisters, a book for my brother, some little trinkets for the kids I teach."

"Nothing he could have put something inside and hidden there?"

She thought about it, running through the list of things she'd brought back. "No."

"Okay. Then I don't know what he's looking for, but I'll figure it out. I swear I will."

Kim nodded.

She was counting on him to do just that, to keep the people she loved safe from the criminal she'd led into their midst.

Chapter Twelve

I hate this job! Nick told himself as he watched her walk away. *I hate this friggin' job!*

He looked around the room in disgust, broken glass on the floor, little bloody paw prints everywhere, a brokenhearted woman beating herself up, now on the way from his room to hers.

He walked over to the window, put both palms against the sill and leaned over it, his head hanging low, hating himself and his job and people like that scum Eric Weyzinski.

He hated hurting nice, pretty, innocent women and making them cry. He wouldn't mind putting his fist through the window right now, but he was already bloody from the fight with the cat and his room already looked like someone had committed a mass murder here. He'd already fired his weapon and scared people once in the past twelve hours. More shattered glass, the potential for more blood and the need for more explanations were not good ideas.

Still, he'd really like to smash that glass.

He lifted his head, saw Kim and the dogs make their way across the side yard from Mrs. Baker's backyard to Kim's and then inside. Watched a dark, shadowy image of her entering her apartment and locking the door behind her, then he looked away. He'd already seen too much through these windows.

He was trying to figure out how to clean up the room, so that maybe it didn't look like a mass-murder scene, when his phone rang.

"Yeah," he said, disgusted with himself and the whole world, then Harry answered.

Harry was laughing. "You shot a cat?"

Nick told him to go screw himself, in less polite language, and hung up on him.

Two seconds later his phone rang again and he remembered that he had to warn Harry and everyone else about Kim.

"Okay, just listen, asshole. Don't say anything and don't you dare laugh, because if you do, I will find you and beat the crap out of you right now. Do you understand?"

Harry hesitated, clearly puzzled by the order not to say anything, and then the question that followed, but finally said, "Okay."

"She knows."

"How?" Harry asked.

"Because I told her. I told her everything," Nick growled.

"Everything?"

"Yeah, everything. I shot the damned cat, so I didn't have much choice."

If Harry wondered exactly how the cat-shooting did that, he didn't ask. "Okay," he said. "How'd she take it?"

"Much better than I expected. She hates herself, not me.

Not us," Nick added quickly, realizing what he'd just given away. That he was concerned about her hating him.

"So...what's she going to do?"

"Get this. She wants to help us catch the guy."

"No way!" Harry said.

"Yeah, she does. She told me so, right after I told her the whole story."

"No way," Harry said again.

"I'm telling you, that's what she said. She's not even really mad at me for lying to her all this time."

"No way!"

"Harry—"

"No, really. There's no friggin' way she could not be mad at you."

"She said she wasn't."

"Well, women say all sorts of things they don't mean. You know that," Harry said.

"I'm the one who's been saying stuff I didn't mean. I've been lying to her."

"No. She may not be mad at you at the moment, but she will be. Trust me on this. Let all this stuff sink in and she'll figure it out. She'll be furious with you."

Nick thought about it and decided that was likely true. That he'd feel better if she was mad at him. Okay, maybe not better, but he felt like he deserved to have her mad at him. Furious at him, actually.

If he hadn't kissed her, maybe it wouldn't have been so bad, so worthy of anger, but he had kissed her, more than once, while lying to her about everything, and women did not take that well. He didn't think they should. It made him a lot like Eric, and every woman should be mad at Eric, so Kim should be mad at Nick, too. It all made perfect sense to him.

"So, what are you going to do now?" Harry asked.

"She's at her apartment, beating herself up for being involved with this jerk. I'm going to let her do that for a while because...well, because I think she needs to deal with the whole thing. And then I'll go talk to her again and figure out where we go from here."

He had to. He had a job to do, which meant, he had to take her up on her generous offer to help them with their investigation. Which he didn't want her to do, because he didn't want her to have anything to do with this jerk anymore or to be anywhere near him. But this, too, was Nick's job, and he would do it.

Which meant, he had to go talk to her, probably explain some more things to her that she really didn't want to know and watch her cry a little more and feel awful and blame herself. He could feel even more like crap for taking part in making her feel this way.

Perfect.

"She just went into her apartment and she's going to stay there for a while. You have people on the house?"

"Yeah. Sure," Harry said.

"Nobody goes in if we don't know who they are, okay? I don't care what kind of excuses you have to make or what you have to do. Nobody goes into that house."

"Okay," Harry said.

"I'm going to be in my room for a while. I've got a mess to clean up here." A jewel of an understatement there.

"Okay."

"Hey, Harry, you know how to get blood out of stuff?"

"Stuff? What kind of stuff?"

"Clothes, sheets...that kind of stuff?" The agency had crews whose sole duty was to make it look like nobody had ever died in certain places, after really messy deaths, but he couldn't very well bring a clean-up crew in here, not without doing some more explaining that he didn't think he could do with Mrs. Baker.

"I don't know," Harry said, then laughed. "Do cats bleed that much?"

Nick swore. "Shut up, Harry."

"Hey, Nickie. Wait… I just have one question."

"Yeah?"

Harry laughed again, laughed hilariously. "Why did you shoot the cat?"

Kim drowned her sorrows in ice cream and let the dogs gorge themselves on anything in her cabinets remotely resembling a dog treat, then sat down on her couch, Petunia in her lap, Romeo curled up against her side. She just sat there and felt sorry for herself for a while.

Maybe she'd just do this for a week or two.

A month maybe.

Whatever it took.

The phone rang a while later and she didn't want to, but she answered it, afraid she already knew what was coming.

Her family.

Had to be.

They'd heard some weird gossipy version of what had gone on at Mrs. Baker's house last night and wanted to make sure she was okay.

She sighed heavily, feeling very, very sorry for herself, then picked up the phone.

At the very last moment before she said anything, she started to wonder if it might be Eric. If he might have finally called, and what she would have done if he had, how she would have handled it.

She was just starting to get really, really scared when she heard her sister Kathie's voice saying, "Kim? Are you there?"

"Hi," she said hurriedly. "Sorry. I almost dropped the phone." She banged the receiver against the side of the sofa for good measure. Too late, but she did it. "Sorry. I did drop it."

"Are you okay?" her sister asked.

"Sure. Why?"

"Because Kate said that Jax said that Mrs. Baker called 911 last night. Something about a break-in—"

"No, there was no break-in. I talked to Mrs. Baker myself." True on the most technical of levels. Kim had talked to her. She'd told her to get rid of the 911 operator.

"So, what was it?"

"A mistake, that's all. She thought she heard something." Again, true. "And called 911." Because Kim told her to, but still…technically true. "But it was nothing."

The secret agent next door just shot a cat. That was all.

Kim wanted to cry again and she wondered how poor Cleo was doing. She'd have to call Mrs. Baker later and check on her, make sure she was okay.

She felt a little bad about the thousand-dollar vet bill, but not that bad. Someone had to pay, and Nick had an expense account. Served him right to have to explain to his supervisors that he shot an innocent cat for no reason. Or…for not much of a reason, Kim decided.

"You're sure nothing happened?" Kathie asked.

Kim's family had a radar about these things. She might be able to put them off for a while, but eventually, they'd find out everything. She knew from experience. With her family, there was no place to hide for long.

"I'm sure. I'm fine. Mrs. Baker's fine. Everyone's fine."

"Okay," Kathie said. "But…is there anything you want to tell me?"

"No," Kim said, sure of that.

"Have you heard from Eric?"

"Kind of,' Kim said. Apparently, he'd broken into her apartment and searched it. Or someone he worked with had searched her apartment. That was kind of like hearing from him, Kim reasoned.

"It's just…we're worried about you, you know?"

"I know." Perpetually worried. Poor baby Kim. Poor stupid Kim.

"And you should know Jax is not happy."

"Okay." She'd been warned.

And Kim knew all 911 calls were taped, thanks to a certain incident in her teenage years, at a party she'd attended where some trouble had broken out, when she'd tried not telling the whole truth to her brother about it. So he was probably pulling the 911 tapes from last night right now, listening to the call from Mrs. Baker's house before he came and asked Kim about it, so he could trip her up on any little stories she might be planning to tell him. He was like that, hard to tell little lies to and get away with it.

"Well, okay," Kathie said, obviously not convinced things were okay. "Hey, how's the art project coming?"

"Great," Kim said. "We're ready to start smashing different colored glass into little pieces."

She had mallets, safety goggles and cloth bags. She had a plan. Put the glass inside the bag and smash it. She thought it would be highly therapeutic right now and highly satisfying. She might do it all herself, just because, not even let the kids help with this part.

Being the teacher had to have some perks.

She needed to do things like smash glass.

"Okay," her sister said. "I guess, that's it. I mean, if you're sure there's nothing else?"

Kim sighed, feeling guilty and annoyed at the same time. They loved her. She knew that. And she loved them. And they'd spent their whole lives looking after her, the baby of the family. When you lost your father to a robber's bullet when you were only two and your mother to cancer when you were still in college, your family tended to be a little overprotective. She got that. She loved them for it.

But sometimes she just wanted them all to go away.

It was even worse since she was in trouble and she'd done something stupid and she probably needed someone to look out for her right now. That just made it all that much harder to take.

"I'm fine. I swear," Kim said, then glanced up and out her living room window, and happened to see…Nick?

She walked over to the window.

Yeah, that was Nick, moving about his room.

She'd never noticed before, but with her shades tilted up to catch the sun and let it in, his room was at a perfect angle for her to look right in. She'd never even thought of the room he was in or that…

Wait a minute.

If she could look right into his window this way, that meant he'd have an even better angle to look down into hers.

He could probably see everything she did in here!

"Kim?" her sister said. "What happened?"

"Gotta go," Kim said, furious. "I'll call you later."

She didn't even wait for a response, just hung up and took off for Nick's.

When he said he'd been watching her the whole time…

He meant, he'd really been watching her!

Watching her drop her jeans and peel off her T-shirt on the way into her bedroom, maybe? Or on the short trip from her bedroom to her bathroom?

She tried to remember the last time she'd done that? Taken a short trip around her apartment only half-dressed.

It was her apartment, after all. She had the shades tilted up, and unless someone was at the perfect angle above her and it was nighttime and her lights were on and someone was in the room where Nick was staying, she didn't think anyone could see much of anything.

But he was at the perfect angle and he'd been there at nighttime and she'd been here with her lights on and without much on her body, innocently heading into her bathroom to take a bath.

And now she was going to kill him!

Nick stripped the bed of the bloody sheets and the quilt, then went through his clothes. The damned cat had gotten to his favorite shirt, his favorite pair of pants, even his socks, dammit. He had practically nothing left to wear.

He dumped it all into a pile, awaiting Harry's instructions on how he might get all of that clean.

If not, he'd have to go shopping.

The quilt would be the only real problem. It looked real and very old. As in handmade.

He'd just have to make up a story about it.

Nick frowned. Or maybe he could just tell the truth, kind of. After the cat did whatever Nick had claim it did to hurt itself, the cat jumped up on the bed and ruined the quilt.

Okay, he could say that.

He'd feel bad about it, but he could say it. He'd buy Mrs. Baker a new quilt.

Could you just buy something like a homemade quilt? Nick had no idea. He'd ask Harry to find out.

That done, it was time to think about cleaning himself up.

He was a mess.

Nick winced as he looked into the mirror. There was a smear of blood along his cheek. No idea how he got that. He washed it off and didn't see a cut or scrape underneath. He had a bruise on the side of his face. No idea about that one, either. Maybe when he'd practically fallen out of bed after he'd shot the cat and was trying to get to the light so he could see what he'd hit. He'd banged his face on the side of the bed, he thought. It had not been one of his finer moments.

The first cut he uncovered was the one on his forearm.

The damned cat had bit him!

Not that Nick could really blame the cat. Nick had shot her after all.

He was still having a hard time believing that one.

"Son of a bitch," he muttered, as he tried to pull the makeshift bandage off.

It was stuck in the mostly-dried blood around the wound and it stung like crazy coming off the inside of his forearm.

Nick would have sworn the cat had taken a hunk out of him, from the way it hurt, but it was just a deep, double-furrowed scrape, not as bad as what he'd done to the cat, he had to admit, trying not to be mad at the cat for taking her revenge.

The scrape started bleeding again, and he couldn't find anything but a washcloth to put over it. One more thing to clean blood out of. *Perfect.*

He needed a first-aid kit and he didn't have one with him.

He was heading for his phone to call Harry back when he became vaguely aware of footsteps coming quickly down the hall. Before he could even react, the door to his room was flung open and Kim came charging in, breathless, cheeks flushed, dogs nowhere in sight.

"What happened?" Nick said, afraid it was something awful, that he'd screwed up and Eric had gotten to her.

"You jerk!" she yelled, shoving him aside and walking over to the window.

"What?" He hadn't done anything since she left that would upset her. Not a thing.

She stopped at the window, stuck two hands in between the slats of the blinds and pulled them in either direction to make a spot she could look through.

Right down into her own apartment window.

"You absolute jerk!"

Okay, Harry was right.

She was mad.

"Ahhhhhhh!" she groaned, then shoved him in the chest with both hands, sending him staggering backward. "So, you've been watching me?"

Nick nodded.

She took a menacing step toward him and shoved him once again.

Back he went, staying on his feet, but barely. "Kim—"

"And when you say you've been watching me, you mean you've really been watching me, right? I mean, I walk around my living room and my kitchen in the morning in my little baby-doll pajamas, because, hey, it's my living room and my kitchen. I have blinds and they're angled up because the sun comes in that way and I like the sun. And when I first moved into my apartment, I looked around and saw that there was no one who could see in anyway, except someone staying in Mrs. Baker's daughter's bedroom, and her daughter moved out years ago. So I was perfectly safe. I could have paraded around naked in my living room if I wanted and there was no one to see," she yelled. "Until you came along!"

She shoved him again and, this time, there was no room to stagger backward, because there was a wall behind him. He bumped against the wall and stood there, with her three inches away, eyes blazing, her hands slapping him in a decidedly girlie way on the side of his arm, like she really wanted to hit him, but this was all she'd allow herself to do. And he should be grateful.

"You, Mr. Secret Agent. Mr. I'm Just Trying to Protect You—"

"Okay, I did it, but I didn't want to," Nick tried. "It's just part of the job, and I mean…I didn't like it, I swear—"

"Liar!"

She smacked him in the face then, her palm connecting solidly with his jaw.

She drew back a step, shook her hand out, like her palm stung from the blow. He tried to take it like a man and not protest.

He deserved it, after all.

When he looked at her, he saw that tears had filled her eyes once again, and she looked not so much mad, as hurt once again.

Dammit.

"Me in my slinky robe? Me wrapped up in a towel, coming out of the shower? Putting lotion all over myself? How could you do that to me?" she cried.

"I'm sorry. I swear I am. We just had to know what was going on in there. He could have been hiding in there. You could have been hiding him and we had to know."

Her tears starting falling then.

"Kim…" He reached for her, and she smacked his hands away.

"I am not the bad guy," he yelled. "I'm a government agent doing my job, which is to try to protect you and everybody else. The other guy, the one you were so crazy about, he's the bad guy. Not me."

"No," she said. "You're just a guy who I thought was my friend. Someone I trusted. Someone I laughed with. Someone I thought was…"

She fell curiously silent, then seemed madder than ever.

"Someone you thought was what?" he said.

"Nice," she said, the word like a smack in the face.

"I am nice. I'm a nice guy. Just ask anybody."

"And honest," she said.

"I'm as honest as I can be and still do my job."

"I trusted you," she cried.

"And I'm sorry about that. I swear, I am."

"Worst of all, you made me like you," she complained. "Why did you have to go and make me like you?"

"I like you, too," he admitted. "I shouldn't. I didn't mean to. Because I knew I was lying to you and I knew you'd end up getting hurt in this whole thing and I really, really didn't want to hurt you. But I couldn't leave you here, waiting for that criminal to show up, either. So there wasn't a whole lot I could do. I had to get close to you—"

"Close to me?" she whispered.

Nick nodded. "To protect you. And I had to get you to trust me—"

"And you did. You're very good at that and you did it."

"I didn't want that man to hurt you any more than he already had," Nick tried to explain.

"So, you hurt me instead?" She nodded. "I get it. Really, I do. I was just stupid enough to trust you both. And you—you just had to be another jerk who lied to me about everything!"

She turned on her heel and stormed out, just as quickly as she'd stormed in.

"*Dammit,*" Nick muttered.

He'd gone and done it now.

He'd made her hate him.

Chapter Thirteen

Later that night Nick sat by his window, as he so often had, and listened grimly to the news Harry delivered.

"I don't know if it was him or not who searched her apartment a few days ago. I'm thinking not. But we picked up a paper trail for an alias that turned out to be him, flying out of San Francisco this morning to Atlanta—"

"Atlanta?" Nick nearly exploded. "How long ago?"

"He landed more than an hour ago—"

"Which means, he could be here any damned minute," Nick said.

"I know. I'm sorry. We just figured out the guy was him. I don't know if he rented a car or what. I don't know what kind. We've got people checking right now."

"Dammit, Harry—"

"I know. I know. I'm sorry. I'm sending a copy of the surveillance photo we got of him at the airport to your laptop right now. He's growing a beard and has colored his hair. It's almost blond now. He got off the plane wearing a pair of khaki shorts down to his knees and a Hawaiian-print shirt, really ugly and bright. He's like a damned neon sign. I don't know what he's wearing now, but he's got to be headed this way."

Which meant Nick had to go see *her.*

Even if she did *hate* him.

He had to talk her into letting him into her apartment.

Even though she did *hate* him.

And he had to stay there, cooped up with her, until either the bad guy showed up or somebody caught him.

Even if she did *hate* him.

He hoped she didn't have the dogs with her. Or Mrs. Baker's hell-bent-on-revenge cat.

The animal trio hating him would make for a perfect evening.

"So…you'll get in there? To her apartment?"

"Yeah, I'll do it. Even if I have to break down the door and tie her up to get her to let me stay there. I'll be inside."

He wasn't leaving her alone with her pirate on the way.

"Okay. I'll talk to you as soon as we pick up his trail. You've got three agents watching the house. Just yell if you need us."

Nick just growled at him as he hung up, feeling good and sorry for himself.

He really hadn't wanted to hurt her. Not that he expected her to believe him.

He didn't expect her to make this easy, either, but it had to be done.

He had a job to do and he was going to finish it, as much for her sake as anyone else's.

And then he'd pack up his clothes, bloody paw prints and all, and leave.

End of story.

He'd never see her again and she'd never have to see him.

She could forget all about him and he'd… He'd…

Well, Nick didn't know exactly what he'd do.

Forget her, too, wouldn't he?

He felt oddly unsettled at the thought.

Of course he'd forget her.

She was just a woman. He'd met tons. He'd forgotten them all and she was just…pretty. Exceptionally pretty. And kind of funny, in a good way. And sweet, in a completely naive way, and kind. But it's not like those things were a damned crime. So what if she tended to trust people, maybe too easily, but maybe just because most people in her little town were trustworthy?

So what?

Trusting people shouldn't be a crime, either.

And yeah, he'd miss her, but again…so what?

Just a pretty woman, he told himself, grabbing his gun, his spare gun, his second spare gun and his phone. The bad guy was coming.

Nick was going.

Finish the job.

Catch the bad guy.

Leave.

Forget about her.

That was his plan. That was always the plan and it had always worked.

It would work again.

Nick was sure of it.

He slipped out of Mrs. Baker's house without running into Mrs. Baker or being accosted by the cat. He hoped the beast was still sedated and would be until he left. Then he slipped across the backyard, signaling to the agent stationed across the street so nobody would come chasing after him or shoot first and ask questions later—like he'd done to the cat—and made it to Kim's door.

Taking a breath, he lifted his hand and knocked.

"Kim," he called out, not wanting to scare her. "It's me."

Surely he was better than the alternative—Eric.

"Go away," she called out through the door.

"I can't—"

"Sure you can. You turn around and walk the other way."

"Kim, Eric landed in Atlanta nearly an hour ago. Let me in."

"So? You can watch from your window. After all, you've got a great view."

"No. He's in town and I'm going to be in there with you until we catch him. Now let me in, before your neighbors get worried and call your brother."

At that, the door down the hallway opened and a young woman stuck her head out. It was all Nick could do not to pull out his gun, before he realized it was likely one of Kim's neighbors.

"I was just about to do that. Call her brother. Maybe you didn't know, but he happens to be the biggest, meanest police officer in this town."

"Yeah, I know," Nick said, trying to look as nonthreatening as possible. "But Kim and I are fine. We've just had a little misunderstanding, that's all."

Kim's neighbor, a tiny brunette, glared at him.

Nick turned back to the still-closed door. "Kim…honey?" She'd really hate him for that. "Your neighbor's worried about you. She's going to call your brother in a minute if you don't open up the door and tell her everything's okay."

She wrenched open the door, looking like a woman about to commit murder herself, grabbed him by the arm and none-too-gently pulled him inside. Then told her neighbor, "Sorry, Lizzie. Didn't mean to take our fuss out into the hall. But you don't have to worry. I am perfectly capable of handling this man all by myself."

"Well, if you're sure—"

"I'm sure," Kim said, closing the door.

Nick stood there, not sure where to go from here, not wanting to make a wrong move and make things any worse than they already were.

Kim stood there, arms crossed, glaring at him.

She was dressed in her slinky robe, hair piled up on her head, cheeks flushed, a fine sheen of moisture on her perfectly soft skin.

He caught a whiff of something in the air…something he'd smelled on her before. Something she put in her bath or the the thing she used to wash her hair or something. That smell was all over the room, wafting out of the open bathroom door, he feared.

Which meant, she'd probably just gotten out of the tub, dammit.

He wanted to lay his head down on something hard and cry or maybe bang his head against whatever he could find.

Her, just out of the bath?

And it was worse now, because he could smell her and her fresh-from-the-bath smell. He had a much better view, here in the room with her, than he had from his own room next door and the sight of her was…

What was the right word?

Agonizing? Good, in a terribly painful way? Giving him all sorts of ideas on which he couldn't act?

"Well?" she asked.

Well?

He was lost. *Well...what?*

"You wanted in, you're in," she said, then stood there, glaring at him.

The robe was a pale, peachy color. It shimmered in the light as she breathed in and out, pretty curves pressing against way-too-thin fabric, making his chest hurt, his throat go tight, making it hard to breathe, to think, to do anything at all. He was afraid to move, afraid to say anything, because whatever he said would be absolutely wrong. He was sure of that.

But they couldn't stay here like this.

"You want to go put something on?" he suggested, his voice sounding odd and tight.

"Why?" she asked.

Why? "Because," he said, at a loss to get out any more than that.

"Because...why?"

"Because you're not dressed," he managed.

"So?"

"So...you run around half-dressed in front of people all the time?"

She shrugged, as if it didn't matter at all. "Nothing you haven't already seen, right, Nick? I mean, no use covering up for you, is there?"

He got it then.

She was still pissed and she was not going to make this easy.

She was going to torment him.

"Okay." He nodded, accepted, thought about begging her to put something on, anything, but doubted she'd do it just because he asked. "I just...need to be here. In the apartment. With you. Just in case."

"Fine," she said.

"Sorry. If anything happened to you while I was supposed to be watching you, I would never... I can't let that happen."

"Fine," she said. "Watch me."

She walked into the bathroom, the robe pooling out behind her as she went. He could just imagine how it looked from the front, the ends of the robe parting, bare legs peeking through as she walked.

He was very, very happy she was going the other way.

Maybe she'd go into her bathroom or her bedroom and just stay there, not have to deal with him at all or him with her.

That would be good.

That would be perfect.

He could handle that....

But no...she was back. Walking toward him, the robe billowing out behind her, indeed parting in front, pretty, bare legs peeking out, just as he'd known they would.

Nick swallowed hard and looked away.

Tried to, anyway.

"Kim, I really am sorry. I swear, I..."

She had a bottle of lotion in her hand, he realized too late, and she stood by the coffee table, propping her foot up so that the robe split high on her thigh, falling to either side of it, while she started rubbing lotion on herself.

On one, perfectly toned and tanned thigh, to be specific.

His mouth went dry.

He coughed or maybe kind of choked, trying to clear his throat.

He wondered just how far she was going to take this little payback of hers? And how he was going to withstand it.

It was like she was moving in slow motion. He wasn't sure

if she was or if his brain had simply slowed down to the point that it could only process so much information at a time. Maybe he was a minute or two behind real time now with what he saw or comprehended.

He saw a dainty looking hand, nails perfectly shaped, not too long and graced by a French manicure, followed the slow drag of that hand up and down her thigh, like a caress.

"Kim, please," he said. "I need to be able to think—"

"So think."

"I have to stay alert."

"You look pretty alert to me," she said.

"For Eric. Alert to someone breaking in here. Not to you and your legs."

She smiled up at him. "All part of the job, right, Nick? I'm sure you can handle it."

Then she went back to working on her thigh.

When her hands moved up under the robe, he started shaking, literally.

It was hard to believe. His heart was pounding.

Maybe he was having a heart attack, he decided. Maybe he was old enough.

He wanted to touch her so bad, it was all he could do to keep from grabbing her and begging her to forgive him.

She'd gotten to him in a way he didn't let women get to him and he was in trouble here. Lots and lots of trouble.

She started working on the other leg, calm as could be.

He thought about his hands replacing hers, smoothing over her skin, lingering here and there, caressing, teasing, touching everywhere. Thought about her aching to touch him the way he ached to touch her.

Could she possibly feel that way? Or was she just mad?

"I have to keep a professional distance," he began.

"Really?"

"Yes. I do. If I'm too distracted by you, I can't protect you the way I'm supposed to, the way you deserve."

"Well, you're all the way across the room, Nick. Surely you've got all the professional distance you need," she reasoned.

"You know what I mean—"

"Not really. I mean…I know I was practically naked, here in my own apartment, feeling safe as could be because it is my own home, and I wasn't safe. You were spying on me. That part, I know."

Her hands crept back under the robe again, moving high along that pretty thigh, in a place he'd love to have his hands, if he could stand it.

"I'm sorry about that. I really am. I was just trying to do my job."

She smiled sweetly at him. "And I'm just trying to keep my skin from getting too dry. That's all. I got a lot of sun on the cruise…. But I guess you know that, right? Because you were watching me there, too. Did you like the bikini, Nick? Because I had to really work up my nerve to put it on in public, but I did it and now, well, I wish I hadn't. What did you think? Was it too much? Or too little, I mean?"

"Please don't do this," he said, ready to beg.

"Why?"

She picked up the bottle of lotion once more, put a dab of it on her hand and then started warming it between her palms. Then her left hand slipped beneath the right side of her robe high along her collarbone, her upper arm, along the top of her breast.

He watched every stroke of her hand beneath the robe, couldn't have looked away if his life depended on it.

Truth was, he'd thought about this more than anyone would

ever know. Thought about her like this almost constantly since he'd first seen her on the ship. He'd tried not to, but what man could spend so much time watching her and not think of her like this?

She was perfect. A physically perfect woman and, even worse than that, she was nice. Really nice. Sweet, even. Happy. Charming. Quick to laugh. Kind to old ladies and wounded cats and grumpy secret agents like him.

She was damned near perfect in every way and he would have cut off his right hand for the right to touch her and have her want him to do it, have her touching him in return, kissing him, letting that robe drop to the floor for him.

"I'm dying here, Kim. What do you want me to do? You want me to say that I wasn't just watching you? That I felt something? That I felt a lot. That I want you? Is that what you want me to say?"

"It would help," she said, holding the bottle of lotion again, ready to go to work on the other side, no doubt.

"Well, I do. I want you like crazy. Satisfied?"

"Not nearly," she said, her chin coming up defiantly, a fine sheen of tears glistening in her pretty, blue eyes before she turned around, presenting him with her back.

He didn't know what she was doing when she held the bottle of lotion up for him to take. He just took it, thinking to put it down on the coffee table.

But then her robe starting slipping off her shoulders.

He was afraid at first that she was going to drop it at her feet, and that he just might die right then and there. Call an ambulance. Call someone else to come watch over her.

He'd just die.

But she didn't drop it completely, just let it fall down the sides of her arm to catch at her elbows, let it ease down her body until most of her back was bare, all the way down to that little indention at the base of her spine.

His breath came in on a hiss and his whole body went tight.

"What are you doing?" he asked.

"My back. I can't reach it all myself and I never seem to have someone here to help me when I need it. Put some lotion on my back, Nick."

He wanted to hang his head and cry, to throw his hands up and say he surrendered. She'd won. He'd do anything she said, if she just stopped tormenting him this way.

He was a jerk. He was a rat. He shouldn't have been looking at her the way he had and enjoying it so damned much and he was sorry. Really, really sorry. He'd go burn in hell right now to try to make up for it.

"I can't do that," he said.

"Sure you can. You just put some lotion on your hands and rub. You've watched me do it enough. You should know how by now."

"Okay, you want me to say I suffered? That it hurt, just to look at you? Because it did. Believe me, I suffered. I feel guilty. I feel like I'm not doing my job the way I should be. I worry about that making me ineffective and you getting hurt because of it. I swear, I've thought of everything."

Except maybe her, standing in front of him, doing something like this for real.

She must be really, really mad and really, really hurt and he had no idea what to do.

It was like he'd developed a split personality because of her.

Part of him was yelling to himself, *Don't touch her! Don't you dare touch her!* And the other part was going, *Are you crazy? This is what you wanted. Get your hands on her now!*

She twisted at the waist, giving him a shot of her in profile, grabbed the lotion bottle and before he could stop her, squeezed out a quarter-sized portion of lotion onto his hand.

He swore softly. She turned back around and just stood there, waiting. All that pretty, smooth skin just waiting for him.

A better man would have walked away.

He was sure of it.

Hell, a better man would never have been caught in a situation like this in the first place. A better man wouldn't have hurt her and watched her the way he'd been watching her, wanting to do the things she was now offering him a chance to do.

Not that he expected it to go much further than this.

She was mad, but she wasn't crazy. Payback wouldn't extend much further than him touching her like this, something to make him uncomfortable, but still not be too personal.

Of course, she was naked under the robe, so he had to admit things were way too personal right now, but still. There was definitely a limit as to how far she'd let him take this.

He had to remember that.

So he'd touch her, just a little, the way he'd wanted to touch her, and think about all the things he could not have. Things he'd remember and regret. Things that would make him wish he'd made different choices, that his life was different and could include someone like her.

He rubbed his palms together, warming them and the lotion before he put his hands on her.

Nothing but fingertips at first.

Honestly, he was scared to do any more than that at first.

She sucked in a breath at his first touch, started swaying a little on her feet. Toward him, in the same way he felt his whole being pulled toward her.

"I'm sorry," he said. "Really, I am."

He flattened his palm against her back low on her rib cage, moving slowly up and down, then stroking, down, down, down, down, down, one side of her back and then the next, stopping at the indention of her waist. He found bits of tension here and there, worked at those spots with his thumbs, his mind racing ahead to what he'd like to be doing—sweet, forbidden things.

"I think I'm going crazy," she said.

"Me, too," he whispered.

"I don't even trust myself anymore—"

"Me neither," Nick said. And a damned fine place that was to be—not even trusting himself to know what to do.

"I think, what am I going to do next? Who am I going to be wrong about next and what's going to happen then? Dammit, Nick—"

"You're not going to be around me or Eric Weyzinski, that's what. Because I'm either going to lock him up or kill him and then I'm going to leave town and you can go back to driving the men around here crazy. No more world-class con men or government agents for you. Just…normal guys," he said. "Good guys. Guys who are lousy at lying, because I've got to say, from what I've heard from the women I've known, most men are lousy liars."

She nodded, her back still to him. "That's true. I always thought that was true. Until this."

"It's still true, Kim."

His hands were at her shoulders, kneading there, working their way down her arms. He had to stop, very, very soon.

There were limits to what a man could do and he was very close to his.

She was too close, smelled too good, looked too great, made him just ache.

But every minute this went on was a minute he got to have his hands on her in ways he never thought he would get to touch her. And it was so sweet.

It was agony.

"Tell me to stop," he said.

"Why?"

"Because I have to stop."

"Do you want to?" she asked.

"God, no."

"Then you don't have to stop. Not yet."

So, it was going to be like a grown-up game of chicken? To see who could stand it the longest without calling a halt to this?

"You've got to know, I won't stop this," he said. "I have a conscience, and I like to think I know right from wrong, but I'm a man, too, and I've never been into self-denial, especially not when it's denying myself someone I've been wanting for way too long. So I won't be the one who backs off. That's going to be you," he told her, her neck, looking delectable as could be, beckoning to him.

"How do you know I'll stop you?" she asked.

"Because this isn't what you want."

"You are so wrong about that—"

"Okay, you might want this, but you're not going to let yourself have it, because I know women like you. You were seduced by a crook you met on your vacation, which I'm betting is very unlike you—"

"Wrong," she insisted.

"No way. I'm not wrong about that. Which means, it'll be a while before you let another guy near you—"

'Wrong," she said again.

"How am I wrong about that?"

She turned her head, so that he saw her in profile, cheeks

flushed, eyes dark and very, very blue, angry but aroused, tempted, absolutely beautiful. "I didn't sleep with him," she said.

"That makes it even worse." Nick groaned, dropped his forehead down to her shoulder and closed his eyes.

She didn't even sleep with Eric?

A guy she claimed she was in love with?

"I'd just met him, Nick," she said, as if that explained everything.

"You said you loved him—"

"On the day we left the boat, at the last minute. Yeah, it was crazy. I knew that. But...I thought he'd come here and we'd have lots of time—to really get to know each other and...well, you know the rest."

Yeah, he knew.

She hadn't even slept with Eric?

He was so happy about that, he could have screamed it from the rooftops. The thought of that slimeball touching her, using her in that way and worming his way into her bed with his lies, had been making him insane.

She had been, too.

He didn't know if they were still playing a wicked little game of chicken or not, but at the moment, he had his face buried in the curve of her neck, doing nothing but breathing in the scent of her, his mouth hovering a half an inch above her skin, just kind of taking everything in. Her smell. The heat of her body. The view he had when he glanced down to the ends of her robe, pulled tight across the top of her breasts, her hands in knots holding on to the material for dear life.

He could have his hands all over her, right now. Could have her naked and writhing beneath him in seconds. He knew it.

He wanted a million different things and they all had to do with her.

Chapter Fourteen

Okay, so her little idea of payback had gone way too far and she should have left it at that.

Honestly, she meant to just to torment him for a few minutes and let that be it.

She could still end it right now, no great harm done.

But there was something in his eyes, something dark and smoky and so intense when he'd looked at her. And she just couldn't.

He'd be gone soon, and if he left tomorrow, she'd never know what this was or what it might have been. Because she'd thought there was something between the two of them, too. Something real. Something more than anything she'd thought she'd felt for Eric, the rat.

Could she make a mistake like that twice? A monumental, colossal, world-class mistake like that twice within a few weeks' time?

Because if she could, she should lock herself away from men for a long, long time. She should just give up, resign herself to a life as a single woman, too weak in judgment to ever be trusted with any man again.

And...well...she wanted more than she and Nick had already had together.

So, she could think of this as an act of courage, one of self-discovery or maybe self-preservation, to see if she needed to be locked away from men for decades or if, maybe, just maybe, she hadn't been that wrong about the man standing in front of her.

She could probably talk herself into thinking of this moment like that, at least for a while longer.

And so she'd handed him the bottle of lotion and told him to rub some on her back.

That hadn't sounded so outrageous.

Naughty, but not outrageous.

Nick Cavanaugh had probably had his hands all over any number of women.

What was one more?

That was what she needed to find out.

If it took him doing things like this to her, well...so be it.

There. She'd almost made what she was doing sound noble.

He'd been still for the longest time. She could have sworn she could feel his gaze locked on her back, could feel heat radiating from his body. That it was like he was pulling her to him with everything except his hands and arms. Rocking on his feet toward her, just to get a bit closer. Battling with himself with everything he had not to do that.

She'd eased the edges of her robe apart, let them slide off her shoulders and halfway down her arms. And then it took what seemed like ages before she sensed movement behind her, heard him rubbing his hands together slowly.

Which meant, he was going to do it. He was going to put his hands on her.

She tensed, bracing herself for the feel of his hands against her back, of how it would be, how he'd do it. Whether he'd linger there, because he couldn't help it or whether he could manage the kind of impersonal touch that would tell her she'd once again been a fool.

He took a step closer. She sensed his hand, right off the surface of her skin, long before he let himself touch her.

When he did, his hand was hot to the touch. Hot and strong and gentle as could be, rubbing ever so slowly and carefully, like a man who never wanted to take his hands off of her.

She closed her eyes, nearly bit her own lip trying not to make a sound. A little, throaty, needy sound.

His was a touch that could absolutely curl a woman's toes.

He went from smoothing on lotion to a light, exquisite massage of her mid-back, and she couldn't help it then. She groaned.

He came even closer.

She could feel his warm breath on her shoulder, him nuzzling her neck with his mouth.

Could she just have his mouth on her? Now? Please?

He asked about Eric and she told him, just told him, not even trying to protect herself or her pride anymore.

She shivered, whimpered, as he teased up and down the side of her neck, his mouth open, lips right there, kind of touching her, kind of not, a whisper of a sensation that raced through her. She felt like she'd drank two glasses of champagne and the alcohol had gone straight to her head and it was spinning or the room was or maybe her whole body.

"Are you still paying me back for earlier," he asked. "Like

you did when you put your hands all over yourself a few minutes ago, or is this something else? Something different?"

"It's not payback," she whispered. "And now you're going to ask me what it is and I just don't know, Nick. I guess, I had to know."

"That I want you?"

"Yes." *That.*

"Because I do and I'm happy to show you. I would have begged for the chance to show you, if I thought it would have done any good," he said. "So I'm just going to do this. Do whatever I want to you and when you're ready for me to stop, you just say so."

He finally opened his mouth and barely, just barely, bit into that spot where her neck melded into her shoulder.

Her knees gave out at the touch and she sank back against him.

He caught her easily with his big, powerful body, one arm coming around her waist, the other holding her chin, holding her face right where he wanted it, so he could keep his mouth buried in the side of her neck, a riot of sensations radiating out from that spot.

It was exquisite, as if her whole body had miraculously developed the power of speech and was chanting, *Touch me. Touch me. Touch me now.*

His arms surrounded her completely. Her head fell to his shoulder and then one of his hands was smoothing, soothing, teasing along her collarbone, that spot at the base of her throat, along the top her breast. His mouth was still nibbling at her neck and she was close enough to him now that she could feel his body harden against the curve of her hips.

"What if...I don't tell you to stop?" she managed. She just

wanted to feel, to believe that something was real and that she wasn't as foolish as she feared.

"You will. I wouldn't get that lucky," he said, even as his hand slid ever so slowly over her breast, over the pucker of her nipple, one finger slowly circling, circling, brushing so softly past it and back again. "But I'm done trying to talk you out of it and trying to talk myself out of it. I'm just going to concentrate on what I'm doing and enjoy it. Enjoy you, inch by inch, a handful, a mouthful at a time."

Even so, it took forever for him to simply take the weight of her breast in his hand, holding it, his thumb rubbing against her nipple in a way that made it ache between her legs.

His mouth was still at work, on her shoulder now, her earlobe, teasing at the corner of her mouth.

Then, like it was a dare, he turned her around and backed her up against the wall, pressing her against it with his body, wrapping her in his arms, finally letting his mouth settle, hard and sure, over hers in long, slow, draining kisses that left not an ounce of resistance anywhere inside of her.

Her breasts swelled so much they actually ached.

He pulled back just enough to give her a smoldering look. "Not yet?"

She shook her head.

He started to take her robe off of her, then gave her a hard, heated stare and shook his head back and forth.

"No. Don't think so. We're going to leave it on this time."

This time?

And then he proceeded to work his way down her body with his mouth, but through the robe.

"Nick," she protested, hands in his hair holding his face against her.

He'd sucked hard on her breasts, teased gently everywhere

else, and his face was currently buried in her belly. She could feel his tongue licking in the vicinity of her belly button.

Okay, things were getting serious here, like a fire screaming out of control.

She was going to stop him, wasn't she?

There was payback and torture and wounded pride to be salvaged as best she could. There was her own innate sense of caution that had always served her well and a general pickiness about men and a bit of reserve, a sense of privacy, and then there was Nick. And how he made her feel and how she was afraid if she stopped him now, she might never, ever feel like this again.

That this was maybe a once-in-a-lifetime kind of thing, that a guy like him wouldn't come around just any old day.

One who could make her want like this.

It couldn't be normal to want like this, could it?

And then his hands were at the back of her knees, working their way up the back of her thighs, his hands under the fabric of her robe, finally.

They settled on her hips, palming them, holding her to him, his face sinking lower. *Oh, my.*

She could feel his breath on her, either through the robe or not, she couldn't tell.

It was all she could do not to sink to the floor.

Her hands caught hard in his hair, holding him to her.

Not that he was trying to get away.

And the robe was still there. She could tell.

But then, it wasn't.

"Ahhhh."

That was just his mouth, nothing between it and her.

She looked down and saw his head working its way in between the gap he was making between the ends of her robe and then his mouth settled on her there. Just his mouth, between her legs.

"I'm going to fall down," she said, sure that she was.

He laughed. "No, you're not. I'm not going to let you."

And after that, he held her hard, hands on her hips, pressing her against the wall so she didn't fall down.

His mouth, in contrast, was impossibly soft, impossibly hot, shockingly intimate.

He finally let her sink down to the floor, then laid her out on her back and buried his face between her legs once again until she cried out his name, gasping for breath, her shoulders heaving, not a shred of self-control or self-consciousness left in her.

It felt that good; she was powerless to stop anything in her reaction to him.

She curled up on her side, trying to hold on to herself, like she might just break into a million pieces if she didn't hold on to herself. Like he'd shattered her. Every bit of her resistance and fears, her doubts and her shyness. Every bit of her reserve.

He stood on his knees, kneeling beside her, pulling off his shirt with an impatience that thrilled her, even as drained and satisfied as she already was, then pulled out his wallet, looking for a condom.

"I'm not fooling around anymore," he said, unzipping his pants, pulling them down, ripping open a condom and putting it on. "Just in case there's any mistake about this. I shouldn't do it, but I don't care. It's what I want and, sometimes, I should get what I want, not just do the things I have to do."

She nodded. He'd brought a condom, even thinking she hated him.

She was very, very happy about that, and she was going to let him do anything he wanted to her. She'd regret it in the morning, if she had to. It wasn't as if she didn't have anything to regret, but none of them had felt anything like this.

He settled himself between her legs, the robe still on her, but pushed aside. He put his weight on his hands on either side of her, looming over her, looking as disheveled and powerful and handsome as she'd ever seen him.

Arrogant, she decided.

The man had a definite arrogant streak and it turned her on.

"Please don't tell me that you've never been with a man," he said.

"No." She took great satisfaction in telling him.

"No, you haven't, or no, you're not going to tell me that?"

"No, I'm not going to tell you that."

His look said he didn't believe her, but it was true.

He was going to find out for himself in just a moment anyway.

"Kim?"

"I have," she insisted, reaching for him.

He settled himself against her with a groan, like it hurt just to touch her this way, and he held the weight of his upper body on his arms as he settled his lower body against hers. She wanted to close her eyes, but couldn't, because she wanted to see his face, too, see how it felt to him. See if she could make him as crazy and out of control as he'd made her.

If she couldn't, she'd just have to keep trying until she could, she decided.

She felt him, big and hard, at the entrance to her body, pushing slowly inside.

It was tight, despite how ready she was for him. She told herself to relax, to just let it be. She wanted him there. Truly, she did. She wanted everything he had to give her.

He made a face and eased a bit farther in, looking down at her like he didn't quite understand.

"Okay, but it's been a while for you, right?"

"Maybe," she admitted.

He groaned. "Kim, let me in."

She let her legs fall open even farther, wriggling and pushing up against him. He was heavy. His body was so hot, surrounding her, as he went deeper and deeper.

It was like what he wanted was impossible for a long moment and then, it wasn't.

He was there, slid into the hilt.

He closed his eyes and gasped, like a man in pain. Serious pain. She wrapped her legs around him, wrapped her arms around him and just held on, on and on. His body rocked against hers, a tiny, tiny movement. How did it feel like so much when he was barely moving?

She felt like she could happily climb inside his body and it still might not be close enough, as if she couldn't hold on to him tightly enough or give enough or do enough. She wanted more, had to have more, had to get him to give her more.

"Nick," she said, trying to tell him.

"Not yet," he insisted.

"Nick—"

"Not yet."

"I want—"

"I know," he said, still barely moving.

"But I—"

"I know—"

"It's too much. I can't stand it—"

"Sure you can."

His mouth was back at that spot on her neck. She loved that spot. And she was moaning, groaning, her hands on his hips, pulling him closer, this little rocking move he was making about to make her insane. And he knew. The man just knew it.

He'd turned her body to liquid, she decided. Like she'd just melted for him. There was a bit of substance and strength left in her arms, to hold on to him, but that was it. The rest felt like a puddle. A puddle of sensations.

She couldn't get enough air into her lungs to satisfy her, couldn't say anything anymore, couldn't think of anything but him and how it felt to have him buried inside of her.

"Nick, make it stop," she cried out finally.

"It will—"

"I can't stand it anymore. It's too much. Too crazy. Too scary. Make it stop."

"I will. I promise. I just—"

And then it started, even more powerful than the first time, her body clamping down on his, as her whole body went tight again and again and again.

"There," he said. "That's it. That's what I wanted."

She cried out.

He did, too, that maddening control of his shattering finally as he moved powerfully, deeply, undeniably.

She lay there, exhausted, trembling, holding on to him as he'd held on to her when he lost all control, driving into her again and again.

When it was over, he collapsed heavily on top of her, his breathing coming in ragged gasps, the pulse thrumming through his whole body and seemingly into hers.

He slowly nuzzled her neck with his mouth, as he had when this whole thing had begun, and she could sense more than see the smile on his handsome face.

"You didn't say stop," he said, as if that still surprised him.

"I know."

"Do you wish you had?"

"I might in the morning, but I don't right now. Do you wish I'd stopped you?"

He laughed. "Do I look like I could possibly be that much of a fool?"

And then she laughed, too.

He eased his body off of hers, pulled her over and tucked her against his side.

"I'm too damned old to do this on the floor," he said after a long, lazy moment.

Which made her laugh again.

"How do you feel about having me in your bed?" he asked.

"Having you there? Or…having you there?"

"Either one. You know what my vote is."

"Well, you're too old to sleep on the floor all night. If we did that, you probably wouldn't be able to walk in the morning and then you couldn't catch the bad guy, now could you?"

"That was mean," he said, rolling off of his back and onto his side, rolling her back onto the floor as he went. He leaned over her, looking as powerful and capable a lover as could be. "And I will make you pay for it. Don't doubt it for a minute."

"Fine," she said. "Go ahead and make me pay."

To her great satisfaction, he did.

Chapter Fifteen

Nick woke up in her bed, naked, with her naked, too, draped over him as bonelessly as a blanket, the robe that he didn't want to take off of her the first time and simply didn't take the time to take off of her the second time, draped over them both.

He'd fallen asleep, exhausted and as satisfied as he'd ever been in his life, not worrying about watching out for bad guys or protecting her or anything at all.

He didn't even know where his gun was.

Anything at all could have happened and here he'd have been, caught literally with his pants down.

Damn, he muttered to himself, reaching for his phone.

He didn't know where that was, either. Somewhere on the floor, he supposed, in the living room, where he'd pulled off his clothes and then fallen on top of her. On the living room floor. Always the gentleman, Nick.

She probably had bruises from that little encounter.

Not that she seemed to mind, judging from the way she was sleeping, melted against him like warm butter.

Naked, warm, sexy butter.

He was waking up in all sorts of places, just thinking about it.

Her draped over him this way, soft, sweet-smelling curves, all that bare skin, her head on his chest, palm flat against his heart.

He fought back the voice of reason and responsibility inside of him that tried to say, *How the hell did this happen?* And, *What the hell were you thinking?* And, *What the hell are you going to do now, Nickie?*

And went for the more practical issues.

Where was Eric? What was Harry doing? What did he know? What should Nick be doing right now to protect Kim from the crook who was out to get her?

He eased over on the bed, drawing a mumble of protest from her, ignoring as best he could the slide of naked skin over naked skin, and went just far enough to reach the phone by her bed so he could call Harry.

"It's me," he said when Harry answered.

"Really? Rough night, Nickie?"

"Yeah. Really tough."

Harry laughed. "You know, Mother worries about you when you don't check in on time and we can't get you on the phone."

"You're not my mother, Harry."

"But I worry. You know that."

"Yeah. Go ahead. Say it." Get it over with, Nick thought.

"Hey, it's no skin off my nose. I mean, if she'd have me, I'd be in her bed in a heartbeat. I'd like to think I would show a little more class and consideration than to have my way with her on the floor, but then, that's just me."

"You watched us?"

"No! I mean, I have my moments, but I wouldn't do that to you—"

"So, you came in here?"

"Just me, just inside the door to her apartment, just barely, when we couldn't get you on the phone. I told you. We worry. But all I saw was your clothes in a mess on the floor, and…well, I could hear that…that everything was okay. I mean…really okay. And then I left. Right away."

Nick closed his eyes and swore.

Harry had been in here? He'd heard them?

And Nick had been so caught up in her, he hadn't even noticed.

"Sounded like you were doing great, Nickie. I'm impressed. Truly—"

"Shut up, Harry."

"I mean, I didn't think guys our age had a chance with someone like her and even if we did, I figured it would take some kind of pharmaceutical assistance to satisfy her. I mean, it would for me. But you…Nickie…I'm so proud."

"I'm going to knock you on your ass the minute I see you."

"Yeah, yeah, yeah. I had to make sure the pirate hadn't slipped past us and gotten into her apartment, didn't I?"

Nick admitted grudgingly that he did.

"Speaking of our bad guy, I do need to see you. We've got to talk about what we're going to do. Weyzinski's holed up in a motel on the edge of town, has been since around midnight. We've got two agents sitting on the place and we need to decide what we're going to do. Wait him out and let him lead us to the diamonds, or what. So if you can drag yourself out of her bed… I mean, I wouldn't. Not for this, but I've always said you were a better man than me, Nick—"

"Name the place. I'll be there," he growled.

"I took a room at the B&B. First floor, opposite the side entrance to your girlfriend's place. I figured with Weyzinski this close, we needed to be closer."

"All right."

"I could come to you, if you like," Harry offered.

"No way," Nick said. He didn't want Harry in this room, with Kim. "Give me ten minutes. I'll come to you."

"So…I get details right? I mean, your love life is as close as I get to a love life these days. It's bad, Nick. Bad."

Nick hung up on him.

Kim was vaguely aware that someone was talking to someone in her bedroom.

Had she left the TV on?

Was someone leaving a message on her answering machine?

She went to burrow deeper into that nice, warm spot in her bed, only to realize, it wasn't just a nice, warm spot.

It was a man.

A naked man.

Nick.

A huge, happy, happy grin spread across her face. She inhaled deeply, taking in the scent of warm, strong, sexy, naked man.

In her bed.

Her grin just got bigger.

She'd gotten him into her bed and he was still here and she was so happy about that.

To heck with feeling stupid and foolish and making bad decisions. She really didn't care at this moment.

She had Nick in her bed.

Nick, the most amazing, sexy lover she could ever imagine.

Yum.

Just yum.

She gave a long, slow sigh and kissed him on the shoulder, the first part of him she saw when she opened her eyes. A blush crept up her body like a heat wave and settled into her cheeks like they were on fire, but she didn't care.

Nick was in her bed.

"I have to go," he said softly, already slipping away.

"What?" She went to scramble after him, nearly losing the sheet that was covering her and only then remembered she was naked—stark naked—and saw that it was morning, bright morning light shining into her bedroom.

He sat on the edge of her bed, his back to her, turning so that she could see his face in profile. "Just for a few minutes and just next door. I have to talk to Harry—a guy I work with. We've got Eric holed up in a motel on the edge of town and we have to talk about whether we're going to go in and get him or wait him out and hope he leads us to the diamonds."

"Oh."

"Don't worry. There are agents watching your building and I won't be long."

"Okay," Kim said.

So…she could just wait right here for him?

Because that would be good. If they were going to stay here in her apartment, waiting Eric out, they could just stay in her bed. That would work for her.

Would it work for him?

Nick turned sideways, bent over and kissed her forehead, pulled back and said, "Should I apologize for last night?"

"I don't know. Are you sorry about last night?" she asked.

He looked as if he wondered if it were a trick question of some sort.

Which was not a good sign.

"You can think about it and tell me later," she said, before he said something she really didn't want to hear and wasn't going to accept anyway.

She wasn't sorry and he wasn't going to be, either.

Looking grim, he stood up, had a lean, hard body worthy of being immortalized in sculpture, minus the cat scratches of course, she decided, looking at the play of muscles in his hips and thighs, all those smooth, hard lines and curves.

Yum.

"I'll be right back," he said. "I'll lock the door behind me. We know where Eric is. You're safe here."

"I know," she said.

She wasn't worried at all anymore.

She eased back onto the mattress and her pillow, the sheet slipping precariously down.

Nick was looking, so she didn't even try to cover herself, just put her arms above her head and stretched languidly, like she didn't have a care in the world. He could watch all he wanted and she'd just stay right here, waiting for him to come back.

He groaned, made a Nick-face, the one he wore to try to convince everyone he was a grump, when she believed he was mostly worried and looking at her like a man who really liked looking at her, but he thought he shouldn't be looking.

She loved that look.

It said she was getting to him.

Nick made himself look as respectable as he possibly could in five minutes for the walk from Kim's apartment to the B&B, not wanting every agent here to know what he'd been doing all night, on the off chance that Harry hadn't already made a general announcement to the troops.

He walked inside, finding no one there except the cat, still bandaged, lounging on a pillow, her nose stuck in the air like she was seven different kinds of royalty and he was a peasant who should be worshipping at her feet.

At least she wasn't hissing at him or baring her claws.

He knocked on Harry's door, then stuck his head inside. "Let's do this in my room. I need a shower and some clean clothes."

Harry, grinning from ear to ear, said, "I ever tell you you're my hero, Nick? I mean, you are my hero."

"Yeah. Don't say another word about her and I might not have to hit you, Harry."

They went upstairs into Nick's room. The bloody bed linens and clothes were still in a pile on the floor. Harry laughed when he saw them.

"Cats? Who knew they had that much blood in their bodies?" Harry said.

"Yeah. If you're going to stay here, take it from me. Steer clear of that cat," Nick said, shrugging out of his shirt and digging through his suitcase for anything that didn't have blood on it that he could wear.

"Geez, Nickie. Is Miss Gorgeous some kind of wildcat in bed?" Harry said, pointing to Nick's side.

Nick looked in the direction Harry was pointing, toward Nick's abdomen, scratched all to hell.

"I told you. The cat."

"Oh." Harry laughed then. "Damn. I know you're the man, but I couldn't figure out what you'd done to her to get her to do that to you—"

"Harry?" Nick pulled out his gun and said, "How about a little pistol-whipping? You up for that?"

"No. I just—"

"Then shut up about her."

"All right. All right. Jeez. I mean, she's just a woman."

Okay, he could kill Harry later, Nick told himself. They had a job to do, catch Eric. And they had to do that so Kim would be safe and for that he needed Harry. But the job would be over soon and then he could do anything he wanted to him.

"I'm getting in the shower. Don't say a word while I'm in there," Nick ordered.

Five minutes, he was in and out, and when he walked back into his room, Harry was gone.

"Harry?" Nick called out. "Come on. Let's just do this."

He heard the cat give a big, loud roar. The thing had the biggest, loudest mouth of any cat he'd ever encountered. Then he pictured the cat sinking its teeth or its claws into Harry and he liked that idea. If it was happening, Nick wanted to see it.

"I told you to stay away from the cat," he called out as he headed down the steps, shrugging into a light jacket, gun tucked into the small of his back.

And walked right in on…

Harry standing in the corner saying, "Sorry, she called me down here and I came, just like that."

Nick turned to the right, saw Mrs. Baker tied up in a chair, looking terrified.

Panning a little farther to the right, there was…Eric Weyzinski, holding a gun on the three of them.

Great.

Was he going to botch this job completely? And what the hell was the guy doing here? At Mrs. Baker's? He slipped away from their agents and then what? Got the wrong address or something? Make a mistake in reading the house numbers?

Assuming he hadn't already been next door at Kim's.

Kim.

"What's going on here?" Nick asked, calmly as he could manage.

"I'm just looking for something. That's all," Eric said. "I just want what's mine and then I'll leave. Nobody's going to have any trouble. Understand?"

Nick nodded. "Sure. What are you looking for?"

"Get over there by the old lady. Now. Both of you."

Nick went. Harry did, too.

"I told him. I don't have anything of his. I don't even know who he is," Mrs. Baker said.

Nick put a hand on her shoulder and told her to let him handle this, that everything would be okay.

"Gun on the floor and kick it to me," Eric said. "Slowly."

Nick did it, thinking about his spare gun and his second spare gun, which he'd left in his room, dammit.

Eric turned back to Mrs. Baker, looking like he was ready to strangle her. "Something from your neighbor," he told Mrs. Baker. "The pretty girl next door, who just got back from a cruise."

"She didn't bring me anything. I thought she might, because she's sweet like that, always bringing me little things. But she didn't this time. I remember the morning she came to say hello to me, when she got back. She didn't have anything with her."

"No. She did get you something. I was with her when she bought it—"

"Well, even if she did, it would be mine. Not yours," Mrs. Baker reasoned.

Eric looked disgusted, impatient. "There's something of mine in the package. That's what I want."

Mrs. Baker looked puzzled, like she just wasn't all there. "Well, I don't know anything about that."

"Kim mailed it. It was kind of bulky and breakable, so she had the man at the shop where she bought it package it for her and mail it directly here. So you would have gotten a package in the mail."

"Oh," Mrs. Baker said. "Well, we've gotten all sorts of packages. We just opened for business and we weren't quite ready. Things just kept arriving. Some of them, I didn't even have a chance to open yet, I've been so busy. You know how that is…."

Eric's look said that he didn't. He was getting more disgusted by the minute.

Nick didn't think it would be that much of a problem to take him down. Harry would cover Mrs. Baker. Harry would know to do that. And Nick would make a flying leap for Eric when Eric let the gun point just a little bit more toward the ground, so that in case he fired, he wouldn't hit anybody.

That was Nick's plan.

Wait and be ready.

Piece of cake, he decided.

This would all be over in no time.

He could go back to Kim and…explain.

Nick frowned.

Explain?

How did he explain?

What did he say?

He was stuck, trying to figure out anything in the world he might say to her when she came running into the room.

"Nick? I remembered. I got Mrs. Baker…" She came to a halt when she saw him and Harry beside Mrs. Baker, tied to a chair.

Nick held up his hand to tell her to stop, right there where she was.

He didn't want her making any sudden moves, didn't want Eric doing anything he'd regret and Kim getting hurt in any way, and he really, really wanted to kill the man right now.

Nick should have found him days ago, should have jumped him a minute ago, so that it never came down to this.

To Kim being in a room with this man while he was holding a gun.

"You sent her a wind chime," Eric said, the gun leveled right at her.

Kim whirled around to face the man, a look of pure fury on her face. "You—"

Nick took two steps forward and grabbed her by the arm.

"Hold it right there," Eric said, aiming at Nick again, thank goodness.

"You rat! You snake!" Kim yelled.

"Just hang on," Nick told Eric, then slid an arm around Kim's waist, picked her up off her feet and didn't set her down until she was behind him, her body shielded by his.

She was so mad she was sputtering, mad about Eric being here and about Nick manhandling her, but he didn't care.

"Stay there, right behind me, and don't move until I tell you to," he told her, as furious as he remembered being in his entire life.

What did she think she was going to do? Take down a man with a gun? While Nick was in the room?

Like he'd ever let that happen.

"I will handle this," he said. "You sent Mrs. Baker a wind chime?"

"Yes," Kim said. "For the B&B."

"In the mail?"

"Yes. I was afraid it would get broken in my suitcase, so I had it mailed."

"To your apartment or her house?"

"Her house. I forgot all about it until this morning. Sorry."

"It's okay," Nick said. "Everything's going to be fine."

He turned to Mrs. Baker. "You don't remember getting a package from Kim?"

She shook her head. "But we've had so many things delivered in the last few weeks."

"Okay. The things that came that you haven't opened yet? Where are they?"

She looked like she was going to cry then. "All over the place."

Nick sighed. It was true. There were boxes here and there, in the corners of most every room downstairs. He could see four unopened packages in this room alone.

"Try a little harder to remember," Eric told Mrs. Baker, taking a menacing step toward her.

She started to cry. Kim yelled at him in outrage.

"Okay, okay. Just relax," Nick said. "Everybody relax. We're going to figure this out. He's going to get his package and leave, okay?"

"You," Eric said to Kim. "You're going to look, and you're going to find it and bring it to me. Everybody else is going to stay right where they are."

"No. I'll do it," Nick said.

"No, you won't. Kim will."

"No," Nick said.

Nonnegotiable.

Every situation like this had certain points that were nonnegotiable and one of his was that Kim was staying behind him, out of the way of that gun.

"Now, the thing you need to understand," Eric told him, "is that I'm the one with the gun. That means I'm in charge here. So here's what we're going to do. We're going to tie you and the other guy up and you can sit in the corner with the old lady while Kim helps me find my package."

"No," Nick said.

"Nick, it's okay. I can do it," she said.

"No."

He was going to jump the guy. He'd have to. That was all there was to it. He turned to Harry, to tell him it was time, to cover Mrs. Baker. Nick was going to shove Kim down onto the floor. It was the safest place for her. The gun would have to be pointed up toward the ceiling, but that was fine, too.

He could do it.

He had to.

"I told you," Eric began, laying out his terms again.

Nick focused on the tip of the gun barrel.

That was the key.

Point it up. Point it away. Anywhere but here.

All he needed was a split second.

Then he saw the cat lurking halfway down the stairs behind Eric's head.

Nick was so surprised, he gave it all away in his face.

"What?" Eric said, worried at the last minute.

The cat had slipped between the railings and was on the edge of a step, nothing between her and Eric's back.

The hair on Cleo's back was standing up on end and she had that look on her face

That attack-cat look.

Her claws came out and she gave a roar of pure outrage.

Next thing Nick knew, the cat took a flying leap, landing on Eric's head, claws sinking in.

He screamed, either in surprise or outrage or pain, Nick didn't know.

Pain, he'd bet.

He remembered those claws.

And it was all the time Nick needed. He shoved Kim down

hard, heard Harry moving to cover Mrs. Baker, and lunged toward Eric. Taking his gun away proved to be easy as could be, thanks to the cat.

Eric howled and tried to shake the cat off, but Cleo had a grip on Eric's neck and face that made Nick wince.

Who'd have ever thought?

Nick, super-secret agent, bested by a cat.

They got the cat off Eric finally, got Eric tied up, and a shaken-up Mrs. Baker untied. She really didn't understand what had just happened, despite Kim's best efforts at explaining.

Three armed agents burst through the door about ten seconds after Nick disarmed Eric. That really shook Mrs. Baker up.

The cat wasn't too happy about it, either.

But everyone was okay.

They had the bad guy.

He hadn't hurt anyone.

And for the moment, Nick had Kim in his arms.

"You sure you're all right?" he said, not caring who saw him or what the hold he had on her said about anything that might have happened between them.

He just didn't care.

She was still shaking and had a reddish spot on her cheek, where she'd hit the floor after he shoved her down, but she was okay.

"Sorry about this," he said, fingering the spot on her cheek.

"It's okay."

"I just had to make sure you were out of the way. I couldn't take any chances on that, and the floor's the safest spot when someone's shooting."

"Okay," she said.

And then he kissed her, just in case he never got another chance to do that.

"God, Kim," he whispered, his mouth against hers.

His head was still spinning from all that had happened. "I'm sorry we let him get this close. It should never have happened."

"It's okay," she insisted. "Everything's okay."

Nick heard a commotion in the other room, shoved Kim behind him again, just in case. Damn, he was jumpy, and he never got jumpy on assignments.

It was probably the local cops. His guys blew their cover when they charged in here in the middle of the morning with guns at the ready.

Time for a lot of explaining.

"You can shoot me or you can let me through right this instant. Those are your choices," someone called out, then roared, "Kim?"

Nick looked at her. "Your brother?"

She nodded.

"Let 'em in, guys," Nick said, then turned to Harry. "Her brother's probably going to kick my ass. As long as he doesn't pull a gun on me, let him do whatever he needs to, okay? I figure I deserve it."

"Nick," Kim said, coming to stand beside him.

He slipped an arm around her shoulders and drew her close, which was only going to make her brother even madder, but Nick didn't care. She was still shaking. They'd face her brother together.

The guy was as big and mad as Nick had feared.

"Kimmie?" he said, taking her right out of Nick's arms and looking her over from head to toe. Then he turned to Nick. "Is she okay? If you hurt a hair on her head, I swear, I'll—"

"Jax, I'm fine."

"No, you're not. Somebody hit you," he said.

"No, I hit the floor when Nick shoved me out of the way, when he jumped Eric."

"Eric? Eric, the love-of-your-life Eric? That guy?"

Kim nodded.

Her brother turned to the guy currently lying on the floor, tied up. "That guy is Eric?"

Kim nodded.

Nick pulled her back to his side, holding her close.

"The guy you were so sure you were in love with, Eric?"

"Yes!" Kim yelled.

Her brother looked like he was ready to explode. "Eric, the one you wouldn't even let your own brother check out for you?"

"Yes," Kim said.

"She didn't need to have anyone check him out," Nick jumped in. "Because she knew who he was the whole time. She was helping us catch him."

Kim made a face at that.

Her brother shot Nick a look, an I-will-kill-you-now-if-you-really-put-my-sister-in-a-position-like-that look. But he'd stopped yelling at Kim and Nick figured that was the least he could do, to try to help her save face with her family and the town.

"Nick—"

"It's okay, Kim. You can tell them now. This is all over."

"Who the hell are you?" her brother said, then did a double take. An I-can't-believe-it double take. "The idiot who shot the cat?"

Nick pulled out his badge and held it up for her brother to see. "Yeah, I'm the idiot. Department of Homeland Security," he said.

Her brother swore. "I'm still gonna kick your ass."

"Yeah, I figured," Nick said.

Chapter Sixteen

Kim's sisters were still hovering around her four days later, still worrying and taking care of her and offering advice and love.

"You were so brave," Kathie said.

"No, I wasn't."

They had to suspect the whole she'd-been-helping-all-along story was a lie, but they'd let it be, telling the whole town that she was a hero. That's what sisters did when you'd done something stupid, like fall in love with a pirate/terrorist and told the whole town about it. Any opportunity to help, they'd use. Like claiming she'd never been in love with the guy at all, just trying to help catch him. And she loved her sisters for that and everything else.

Her brother was still a little crazy and he'd given Nick a huge black eye, but the X-ray showed Nick's nose wasn't broken, so things weren't as bad as they could have been.

They'd found the package with the diamonds, all there, safe

and sound, and Eric was somewhere in federal custody. Things had gone really well, all things considered.

So what if Nick hadn't touched her since that day at Mrs. Baker's.

So what if he was supposedly leaving town tomorrow and hadn't said so much as three words to her in days?

Kim blinked back tears.

"Oh, honey," Kate said. "You're really crazy about that guy Nick, aren't you?"

Kim nodded miserably.

"Well, what are you going to do about it?" Kate, ever the practical one, asked.

"I don't know," Kim said. "I can't even get him alone long enough to talk to him about anything."

"Well, you can't just let him leave," Kathie said.

"I know, but I don't know what to do," Kim said, then happened to glance out her window and catch a glimpse of Nick.

Nick, who was still in his room at the B&B. He'd been watching her. When she looked up at him, he looked guiltily away. It was almost nighttime. Darkness was falling.

And he was leaving tomorrow?

"Okay, maybe I do have an idea," Kim said, standing up. "And you guys have to leave. Right now."

"Huh?" they said. "What?"

"Now. You have to go right now, before I lose my nerve and chicken out."

She hustled them out the door, deliberately left the door unlocked and ran into her bathroom, wondering if she had the nerve to take this as far as she might have to take it.

She supposed she had to.

Or risk losing him forever.

And Kim wasn't losing him.

* * *

Nick had packed his things, smoothed things over as best he could with the locals, considering her brother could have cheerfully killed him for involving his sister in anything this dangerous.

Mrs. Baker was hovering, grateful and apologizing for misplacing the package and telling everyone who would listen what a hero her cat was, that it was the cat who'd saved the day, not Nick. She still didn't quite comprehend that Nick had shot the cat and Nick hoped she never did.

Cleo, for her part, had developed what Nick would swear was a smirk, an I'm-so-clever, I-made-you-look-like-a-complete-idiot-and-everyone-loves-me smirk that she wore only around Nick.

And she was around Nick a lot, stretched out on his bed at the moment, purring and grooming herself like the silly, pampered creature she was.

Still, Nick had to admit, she made a great attack-cat, and you had to respect that in anybody. Especially one who saved a woman like Kim from scum-of-the-earth Eric Weyzinski.

So he sat down on the bed by the cat, who seemed willing at the moment to grant him an audience, queen-like creature that she was.

Yes, her look said. *You may admire me now, and you definitely owe me an apology.*

She stretched, showing him her still-bandaged paw, laying the guilt on thick.

"Yeah, yeah, I know. I'm sorry. Really, I am," Nick said. "And you have to know I will never, ever, ever hear the end of this. I will go to my grave with people laughing behind my back and probably to my face, telling everybody about the night I shot a cat. So…you know, I'm suffering here, too."

Cleo held up her paw, as if to point out that her suffering had been much greater than his.

"You're right," Nick said, surrendering completely. "You had it worse. You were completely in the right and I was in the wrong. And that takedown on Weyzinski? It was a thing of beauty. Perfect timing and an absolutely gorgeous move. The guy didn't stand a chance. And what you did to his head?"

Nick laughed just thinking about it.

The guy had claw marks all over him. When they'd taken him to the federal building in Atlanta for questioning, the agents in charge didn't believe them for a second when Nick claimed they hadn't roughed up Weyzinski or even tortured him, that the cat was the only one who touched him.

"So yeah, you're all right," Nick said. "For a cat. And…maybe cats are far superior to human beings. Who knows? I wouldn't argue with you about that right now. I'm just glad you were there to help."

Cleo gave a little purr that sounded supremely self-satisfied.

Nick patted her gingerly on the head. "Nice kitty," he said.

She let him, not even trying to claw him or looking haughty or scary, simply a bit dismissive, then rolled over and went to sleep right in the middle of Nick's bed.

He considered that a victory.

He and the cat were buddies, of sorts.

He looked up and saw Harry standing in the doorway to his room, an odd look on his face. "Were you just talking to the cat?"

"What if I was?" Nick said.

"Okay," Harry said. "Fine. Whatever. You packed?"

"Yeah," Nick said, trying not to sound too miserable about it.

"Still haven't seen her?"

Nick shook his head. "What's the point?"

How much could one man apologize?

"I don't know," Harry said. "You could at least talk to her."

"Nothing left to say," Nick said.

Harry nodded, eased into the room and then did a double take as he looked out the window.

"Let me guess," Harry said. "She wants to talk to you, but you've been refusing?"

"Yeah? So?"

"I think she's done asking nicely, Nickie."

"Huh?" Nick said.

"I think, she's not taking no for an answer this time. Jeez, you are one lucky son of a bitch."

"What?" Nick came to stand by the window, looking out at whatever Harry was looking at.

Looking at Kim, he realized.

Kim standing by her window, perfectly illuminated, in her robe fresh from the bath, looking up at him, smoothing lotion on her neck, then down, inside the edges of her robe as it slipped lower and lower and lower.

"Holy—"

Harry got nothing more than that out before Nick shoved him away from the window, then out the door, Nick jamming the lock on the door once it was shut.

"If you get back in this room and look back out that window, I'll strangle you dead. Got it?"

"I don't think I'd survive another look out that window," Harry said. "My heart isn't all that good and my cholesterol's way too high."

"I'd still kill you. I'd kill you again. Understand?"

"Understand," Harry said. "You lucky son of a bitch."

"Don't I know it," Nick said, taking off running out the side door, across the yard and into Kim's building.

He was breathing hard once he got there, slamming her door behind him once he got in, then locking it. He went to the window and closed the blinds tight, while she stood there in front of him smiling, with her hands all over herself, the robe sitting precariously low on her pretty shoulders.

"What are you doing?" he asked.

"Inviting you over," she said.

Nick threw his head back and groaned.

"I don't want you to go," she said.

"Sure you do."

"No, I don't."

"Kim—"

"I mean, if none of this really meant anything to you and you don't really care about me and you can just walk away and not look back, then fine. Go. But I don't believe you really feel that way. I don't think I'm wrong this time. I think I'm right. I think you care about me."

"Of course I care about you."

"I think you're crazy about me," she claimed.

To which, he had no idea what to say.

"Your brother hates me," he said finally.

"So? He hated both my two sisters' husbands when he first met them. It's kind of a tradition. And he threw Kathie's husband through a plate-glass window once, so a little black eye is nothing."

"I'm…my knee hurts. A lot," he said.

"Awww."

"Not from anything your brother did. It just hurts. And my shoulder. And sometimes, my back."

"Poor baby."

"I'm old," he said, in case she just didn't get it.

"No, you're not."

"Fourteen years older than you."

"So? You're funny and you were so nice, telling everybody I knew all along what Eric was and was just trying to help. That was really nice, Nick. You have a gorgeous body, you're great in bed and you took good care of me when I needed it."

"Danger," Nick said. "Big aphrodisiac, danger."

"Okay. Prove it. Come to bed with me, now that it's all over, and let's just see how it goes."

He groaned, like the idea really, really hurt him.

"I mean, if it was all a mistake, let's figure it out now," Kim said. "If you don't want to be with me—"

"I want to be with you more than I want my right arm to stay attached to my body," he said. "I'd fight off hordes of angry cats to be with you, face down an army of pissed-off overprotective brothers, if that's what it took. I just... Are you sure this is what you want?"

She gave him a look of pure joy. "Do you think I'd practically strip in front of my window for just anybody?"

"I hope not," he said.

"I think, and I'm scared to even say it, because I was so wrong before and it all happened so fast and maybe you think I'm ridiculous and silly and stupid—"

"I would never think that about you."

"But, well, I think I might be in love with you," she said.

"Oh, Kim—"

"And if that's not what you want, you have to say so, right now."

"I can't say I don't love that whole idea and all the possibilities that come along with it. But wanting it and thinking it will work are two different things—"

"Well, you could just stay here for a while. We could…get to know each better, see how you like it here, see how things go. You know? It doesn't have to be a whirlwind thing and it's not a vacation fling, because I'm not on vacation anymore. And you're not on vacation, right?"

"No. I mean, I could be. I could take a vacation, if I wanted to. I never take a vacation."

"Just take some time off," she said. "Nobody has a time-off fling or a time-off romance, right?"

"Right," he said.

"And there's no more danger, right? So it's not the danger thing. We could just stay here and have a plain, old-fashioned, boring, getting-to-know-you kind of relationship."

"I don't think you could ever be boring," he said.

She grinned at that, put her arms around him, kissed him with her soft, sweet mouth.

"And you think you might be falling in love with me. Go on. Say it," she told him.

"I've never been in love before, Kim. How would I—"

"Say it," she insisted. "If you think you might feel it, just say it."

"Okay, yeah. I think I might be falling in love with you."

She grinned. "Now we're getting somewhere."

"I've never stayed anywhere in my life for long. I've never had anything that lasts."

"Well, I've been here my whole life. I know all about staying. All about things that last. I could teach you all about it," she offered. "If that's what you want."

"I want," he said, putting out a hand, touching her cheek, her hair, pulling her closer. She was real and she wanted him.

"Good," she said. "Then I think you should take me to

bed, so we can start figuring out exactly how we feel about each other."

And that's what he did.

* * * * *

Mediterranean Nights

Join the guests and crew of
Alexandra's Dream, *the newest luxury ship to*
set sail on the romantic Mediterranean,
as they experience the glamorous world of cruising.

A new Harlequin continuity series
begins in June 2007 with
FROM RUSSIA, WITH LOVE
by Ingrid Weaver

Marina Artamova books a cabin on the
luxurious cruise ship Alexandra's Dream,
when she finds out that her orphaned nephew
and his adoptive father are aboard.
She's determined to be reunited with the boy...
but the romantic ambience of the ship and
her undeniable attraction to
a man she considers her enemy
are about to interfere with her quest!

Turn the page for a sneak preview!

Piraeus, Greece

"There she is, Stefan. Alexandra's Dream." David Anderson squatted beside his new son and pointed at the dark blue hull that towered above the pier. The cruise ship was a majestic sight, twelve decks high and as long as a city block. A circle of silver and gold stars, the logo of the Liberty Cruise Line, gleamed from the swept-back smokestack. Like some legendary sea creature born for the water, the ship emanated power from every sleek curve—even at rest it held the promise of motion. "That's going to be our home for the next ten days."

The child beside him remained silent, his cheeks working in and out as he sucked furiously on his thumb. Hair so blond it appeared white ruffled against his forehead in the harbor breeze. The baby-sweet scent unique to the very young mingled with the tang of the sea.

"Ship," David said. "Uh, *parakhod*."

From beneath his bangs, Stefan looked at the *Alexandra's Dream*. Although he didn't release his thumb, the corners of his mouth tightened with the beginning of a smile.

David grinned. That was Stefan's first smile this afternoon, one of only two since they had left the orphanage yesterday. It was probably because of the boat—according to the orphanage staff, the boy loved boats, which was the main reason David had decided to book this cruise. Then again, there was a strong possibility the smile could have been a reaction to David's attempt at pocket-dictionary Russian. Whatever the cause, it was a good start.

The liaison from the adoption agency had claimed that Stefan had been taught some English, but David had yet to see evidence of it. David continued to speak, positive his son would understand his tone even if he couldn't grasp the words. "This is her maiden voyage. Her first trip, just like this is our first trip, and that makes it special." He motioned toward the stage that had been set up on the pier beneath the ship's bow. "That's why everyone's celebrating."

The ship's official christening ceremony had been held the day before and had been a closed affair, with only the cruise-line executives and VIP guests invited, but the stage hadn't yet been disassembled. Banners bearing the blue and white of the Greek flag of the ship's owner, as well as the Liberty circle of stars logo, draped the edges of the platform. In the center, a group of musicians and a dance troupe dressed in traditional white folk costumes performed for the benefit of the *Alexandra's Dream*'s first passengers. Their audience was in a festive mood, snapping their fingers in time to the music while the dancers twirled and wove through their steps.

David bobbed his head to the rhythm of the mandolins. They were playing a folk tune that seemed vaguely familiar, possibly from a movie he'd seen. He hummed a few notes. "Catchy melody, isn't it?"

Stefan turned his gaze on David. His eyes were a striking shade of blue, as cool and pale as a winter horizon and far too solemn for a child not yet five. Still, the smile that hovered at the corners of his mouth persisted. He moved his head with the music, mirroring David's motion.

David gave a silent cheer at the interaction. Hopefully, this cruise would provide countless opportunities for more. "Hey, good for you," he said. "Do you like the music?"

The child's eyes sparked. He withdrew his thumb with a pop. *"Moozika!"*

"Music. Right!" David held out his hand. "Come on, let's go closer so we can watch the dancers."

Stefan grasped David's hand quickly, as if he feared it would be withdrawn. In an instant his budding smile was replaced by a look close to panic.

Did he remember the car accident that had killed his parents? It would be a mercy if he didn't. As far as David knew, Stefan had never spoken of it to anyone. Whatever he had seen had made him run so far from the crash that the police hadn't found him until the next day. The event had traumatized him to the extent that he hadn't uttered a word until his fifth week at the orphanage. Even now he seldom talked.

David sat back on his heels and brushed the hair from Stefan's forehead. That solemn, too-old gaze locked with his, and for an instant, David felt as if he looked back in time at an image of himself thirty years ago.

He didn't need to speak the same language to understand exactly how this boy felt. He knew what it meant to be alone and powerless among strangers, trying to be brave and tough but wishing with every fiber of his being for a place to belong, to be safe, and most of all for someone to love him….

He knew in his heart he would be a good parent to Stefan. It was why he had never considered halting the adoption process after Ellie had left him. He hadn't balked when he'd learned of the recent claim by Stefan's spinster aunt, either; the absentee relative had shown up too late for her case to be considered. The adoption was meant to be. He and this child already shared a bond that went deeper than paperwork or legalities.

A seagull screeched overhead, making Stefan start and press closer to David.

"That's my boy," David murmured. He swallowed hard, struck by the simple truth of what he had just said.

That's my *boy.*

"I can't be patient, Rudolph. I'm not going to stand by and watch my nephew get ripped from his country and his roots to live on the other side of the world."

Rudolph hissed out a slow breath. "Marina, I don't like the sound of that. What are you planning?"

"I'm going to talk some sense into this American kidnapper."

"No. Absolutely not. No offence, but diplomacy is not your strong suit."

"Diplomacy be damned. Their ship's due to sail at five o'clock."

"Then you wouldn't have an opportunity to speak with him even if his lawyer agreed to a meeting."

"I'll have ten days of opportunities, Rudolph, since I plan to be on board that ship."

* * * * *

Follow Marina and David as they
join forces to uncover the reason behind
little Stefan's unusual silence,
and the secret behind the death of his parents….

Look for From Russia, With Love
by Ingrid Weaver
in stores June 2007.

NASCAR

In February...

Collect all 4 debut novels in the Harlequin NASCAR series.

SPEED DATING
by *USA TODAY* bestselling author Nancy Warren

THUNDERSTRUCK
by Roxanne St. Claire

HEARTS UNDER CAUTION
by Gina Wilkins

DANGER ZONE
by Debra Webb

On sale February 2007

And in May don't miss...

Gabby, a gutsy female NASCAR driver, can't believe her mother is harping at her again. How many times does she have to say it? She's not going to help run the family's corporation. She's not shopping for a husband of the right pedigree. And there's no way she's giving up racing!

SPEED BUMPS *is one of four exciting Harlequin NASCAR books that will go on sale in May.*

SEE COUPON INSIDE.

www.GetYourHeartRacing.com

NASCARMAY